[redacted]

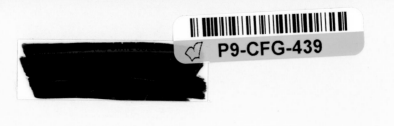

THE
HAUNTED
MOUNTAIN

Also by Mollie Hunter

THE THIRTEENTH MEMBER

THE WALKING STONES

THE
HAUNTED
MOUNTAIN

by MOLLIE HUNTER

Illustrated by LASZLO KUBINYI

A Story of Suspense

HARPER & ROW, PUBLISHERS
New York, Evanston, San Francisco, London

THE HAUNTED MOUNTAIN

Printed in the United States of America. For information address Harper & Row, Publishers, Inc., 49 East 33rd Street, New York, N.Y. 10016.

Library of Congress Catalog Card Number: 77-183164

Trade Standard Book Number: 06-022666-8
Harpercrest Standard Book Number: 06-022667-6

FIRST EDITION

To Robin Murdoch:
fellow-Scot, and mutual friend
of MacAllister and myself.

CONTENTS

THE
HAUNTED
MOUNTAIN

1

THE GOODMAN'S CROFT

Away in the north of Scotland, in the part they call the Highlands, there is a mountain by the name of Ben MacDui, and this mountain is haunted.

There is no doubt whatsoever that this is the case. Everyone knows it to be so, and the creature that roams there is called the Great Gray Man of Ben MacDui. Or sometimes it is called *An Ferla Mor*, which is a name from the old Gaelic language of the Highlands, and which also means the Great Gray Man.

There is some doubt, however, over who the Gray Man is and how he came to haunt Ben MacDui; and so to settle the matter once and for all, it is time to tell the story of a man called MacAllister who lived long ago in these parts.

This MacAllister, they say, was the most stubborn man

that ever drew breath. Also, it seems that he had given offense at one time to certain creatures with a name that is sounded "shee," although it is spelled "*sidhe*" in the Gaelic. "Fairy people" they would have been called in English; but the *sidhe* of the Highlands were not at all as fairies are sometimes imagined to be.

They were small, certainly—about the height of a twelve-year-old boy, they say—and they were beautiful; but they were also a lordly race, and terrible when angered. Moreover, they were both powerful and numerous in MacAllister's time, and all this was a source of great danger to him.

He was a young man then, of course, which helps to explain his rashness, but the real root of the matter lay with a girl called Peigi-Ann Mackenzie. MacAllister was anxious to marry Peigi-Ann, and he might well have persuaded her to take him, too, for he was a big handsome fellow, dark and strong as a pine tree. Marriage, however, meant at least one more mouth to feed, and the bit of land he farmed in a glen some miles from Ben MacDui was poor, stony soil.

MacAllister therefore began casting around for ways to improve the yield of his farm, and it was then that he decided to plow a certain small part of it which had never before been plowed or planted or used for the grazing of animals, and which was called the Goodman's Croft.

Now it was the custom in those days for every man to have a Goodman's Croft on his farm, and this custom arose from the people's fear of the *sidhe;* these creatures being so quick to take offense and so revengeful that it was considered wise to keep in their favor by giving them this croft, or little piece of land, to use in any way they might desire. It was the custom also never to risk offending the *sidhe* by speaking aloud of them, except by pleasant names such as the Good People, or the Good Neighbors; and this, of course, was how the gift of land came to be known as the Goodman's Croft.

To say the least of it then, MacAllister's decision was a foolish one. The people of his glen were quick to tell him so, but MacAllister was much too stubborn to change his mind once he had come to any sort of decision. The land was his to do with as he chose, he argued. Moreover, it had been in his family for more generations than anyone could count, and MacAllister after MacAllister had spent toil and sweat on it.

"Why then," he asked, "should I give up so much as an inch of it to creatures that have never done a day's work in their lives?"

This seemed a reasonable enough argument to MacAllister, but his neighbors were not concerned with reason. "The land is yours, right enough," they agreed, "but you must let the Good People have the use of it."

"There is as much sense to that," MacAllister retorted, "as there would be in giving a hungry man bread and telling him he may not eat it."

"But it is the custom to let the Good People have the

land," they persisted, and one old woman added,

"And a sensible custom, too, for they might put their spite out on the rest of the land if this little bit is not freely given to them."

"That is nothing but a piece of blackmail," MacAllister declared. "And I will not yield to blackmail."

"Then you will have much to fear," the old woman said.

She was a Skeelie Woman, as they call fortune-telling women in these parts, and everyone listened respectfully when she said this; but MacAllister refused to be impressed.

"What have I to fear," he demanded, "from creatures that dare not show their faces in daylight? A man may farm his land in peace, I hope, without shadows to frighten him."

The Skeelie Woman looked strangely at him with her small, glittering eyes, and MacAllister tried to shrug off the uneasy feeling this gave him, for she was a strange-looking woman at the best of times—not like the rest of the folk in the glen at all, in fact.

She was smaller than they were, to begin with, and not fair-skinned as they were, but brown as old leather. She was fond of bright, glaring colors, too, not the soft gentle ones the women of the glen wove into their tartans; and with these bright clothes she wore silver buckles on her shoes and silver rings in her ears. These silver rings were swinging now as she looked up at MacAllister, shaking her head and saying,

"You have the dark to fear, of course. And other things too, MacAllister, for you know as well as I do that the Good People have an ancient magic at their command."

Now MacAllister was normally a very pleasant, cheerful fellow; but like most stubborn men, he was inclined to lose his temper when people argued against him. Besides which, the Skeelie Woman had made him nervous, and so now he exclaimed loudly,

"Ach away, woman! There is no need for any Christian man to fear the old magic!"

"And there is no need for you to bawl and shout just because you get a friendly warning," the Skeelie Woman retorted.

"I am not bawling and shouting!" MacAllister roared at her. Then, so completely had he lost his temper by this time that he did something no one else had ever dared to do before; and that was to name the Good People aloud by their true name.

"Let the *sidhe* come at me as they will," he declared. "I am ready for them!"

Without pausing to argue any further then, he harnessed up a little brown shelty, which was a good plowhorse and just the right size for turning at the end of each furrow in a small field, and set this shelty to plow the Goodman's Croft. Then he harrowed the ground, sowed it with barley seed, harrowed it again, and rolled it flat until it was as neat a little field as you might see in a day's march.

MacAllister looked at the finished effort and compared it with the ugly patch all choked with thistles and dockens and coarse grass that had been there before. It was a good farming job done in a proper and sensible manner, he told himself, and he should get four, maybe even five, grains of barley for every one he had sown. Moreover, not a thing had happened to disturb him while he was working on the Goodman's Croft; and so, feeling quite pleased with the improvement to his farm, he went off to visit his Peigi-Ann.

Peigi-Ann had hair the color of a summer sunrise, all red-gold and shining. Her skin was as white as a drift of white hawthorn blossom; her eyes were the deep, dark blue of the wild hyacinths that bloom under the pine trees in the month of May; and she was the darling of Mac-Allister's heart. Peigi-Ann, however, was a girl with a mind of her own, and when she heard about the plowing of the Goodman's Croft she told MacAllister she would have nothing more to do with him until she heard the outcome of it.

"Because," said she, "there is no one crosses the Good People without peril to his life. And though I am old enough to marry, I am too young to be a widow."

"There will be no outcome except a good crop of barley," MacAllister told her. "And there is no woman will tell me what to do with my land, any more than the *sidhe* will."

So a quarrel sprang up between them, and this quarrel grew and grew until Peigi-Ann told MacAllister she never wanted to see him again. This put an end to MacAllister's courting, for the time being at least, since he was too stubborn to give in even to Peigi-Ann; and so the time he would have spent with her that spring he used instead to go hunting with his hound, Colm.

This Colm was only a young dog, but already he was a great tall creature, lean, and long in the leg, with a rough gray coat and a narrow head—the very spit, in fact, of the hounds in the hero tales of long ago. *An Cu Mor*—the Big Dog—was the name the folk of the glen had for him, and so swift was he in the chase that a saying had grown up among them, "If the March wind can run fast, An Cu Mor can run faster."

MacAllister loved the creature almost as much as he loved Peigi-Ann, and in the weeks following his quarrel with her, he and Colm roamed all over Ben MacDui and the other great mountains of the Cairngorm range. Cairntoul and The Devil's Peak, Braeriach and Ben MacDui's sister-peak, Cairngorm itself, all saw MacAllister's foot that spring; but although he enjoyed good hunting on them all, his heart was still sore for Peigi-Ann and he only kept himself busy like this to show she would not get the mastery over him.

"When the barley shoots green out of the Goodman's

Croft," he thought, "and still there is no sign of trouble from the *sidhe*, then surely Peigi-Ann will admit she is in the wrong and let me come courting again." But the barley grew and ripened into gold, and still MacAllister had no word or sign from his Peigi-Ann.

Neither had there been any hint of danger from the *sidhe*, however, and so one day MacAllister cut the barley and threshed it, after which he found he had enough grain to fill two big sacks. He put the grain into these sacks and was standing in his barn admiring the result of his work when a shadow fell across him. MacAllister looked up to find the cause of the shadow, and there in the doorway of the barn stood an Urisk.

Now an Urisk is quite a frightening sort of creature to see, because its upper half is that of a man, but from the waist down its form is that of a goat. It is also a very surly creature, and immensely strong; but it avoids humankind as a rule and makes its home in some lonely cave on a mountainside. The tribe of the Urisk, moreover, is well known to be in the service of the *sidhe*; and so, as soon as MacAllister saw this one, he knew he was in for the reckoning over the Goodman's Croft. He put a bold face on it, all the same, and roughly he asked the Urisk,

"What brings you here then, Hairy One?"

"Fine you know that," the Urisk growled in its deep voice. "The *sidhe* have sent me, MacAllister, and it is these two bags of barley they want."

"The barley belongs to me, for it was grown on my

8

land," MacAllister told him, "and so you can tell your masters, Urisk."

"What comes from the Goodman's Croft belongs to the Good People," growled the Urisk, and started forward to pick up the bags of barley.

MacAllister gave a shout of anger at this and rushed to stand in front of the bags, but the Urisk simply raised one hairy arm and gave him such a blow that he was sent crashing to the floor of the barn. Then it swung the bags of barley onto its shoulders and made away up the hill above MacAllister's farm, clattering along on its hooves at a fast pace.

MacAllister picked himself up off the floor and ran outside shouting after the creature, but he might as well have called to the wind for all the use that was. The Urisk galloped on with the barley bags bumping on its great broad shoulders, and MacAllister knew there was only one creature on earth could catch it.

"Colm!" he yelled at the top of his voice, "Colm!" And An Cu Mor came running to him.

"After him, Colm!" MacAllister shouted, pointing toward the Urisk. "On boy, on!" And Colm went after the Urisk.

Like the wind he ran; like a gray shadow moving over the hillside; and soon he was snapping at its heels, for even without the barley to weigh it down it could not have escaped such a pursuit.

The Urisk turned at bay, snarling, and dropped the

bags of barley to lunge at Colm's throat with its great strong fingers spread out to choke him. Colm sidestepped nimbly and circled the Urisk, his teeth nipping at the creature's hairy fetlocks. The Urisk lashed out with its hooves and whirled to face him again when the kick missed its mark. And so it went on, with the Urisk lunging and kicking but always missing the nimble Colm, and Colm always circling for another nip.

The Urisk could neither outdistance Colm nor could it break free from the snapping circle the hound's teeth were weaving around it, and so it was held pinned to the one spot until MacAllister should arrive; which he did eventually, red-faced and panting from hurrying up the hill, and with his dirk held ready in his hand.

The Urisk growled fiercer than ever when it saw the bare, shining blade of the dirk, for it thought MacAllister meant to kill it; but MacAllister was not the man to kill something that was even half human for the sake of two bags of barley. Besides which, he realized that the *sidhe* would certainly try some other way to rob him if he killed the Urisk, and so it was another purpose altogether he had in mind.

With a shout and a great sweep of his arm, he plunged the dirk down toward the sacks of barley and ripped them both open. The grain spilled out in two golden heaps from the sacks, and like a man demented MacAllister began kicking it about all over the place. The Urisk watched

10

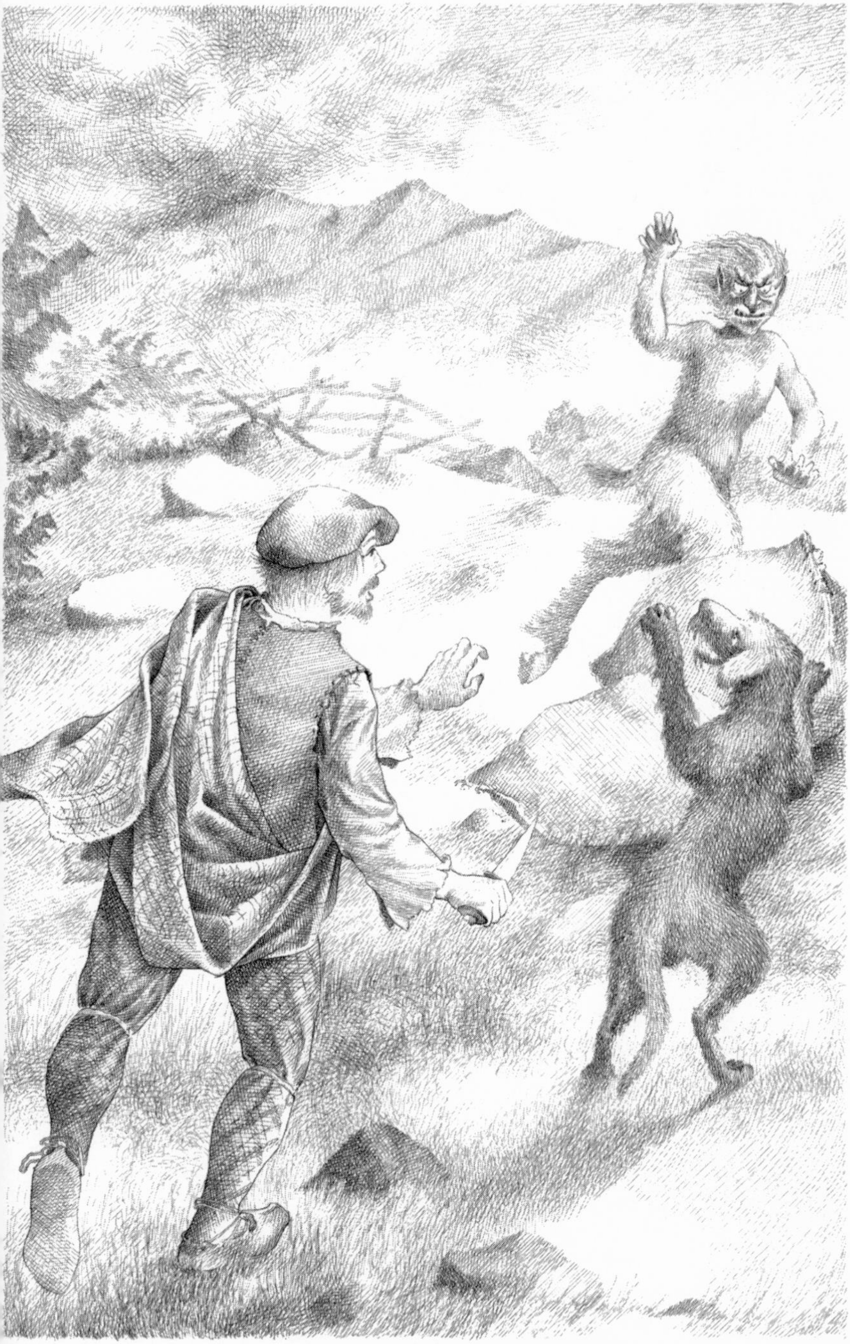

with amazement on its great stupid face, and MacAllister bawled angrily,

"Gape away, Hairy One! I am not so daft as you think I am, for if *I* cannot have the barley, I will make sure the *sidhe* cannot have it either."

He gave one last kick to the barley, and finished, "There! Now let the *sidhe* try to rob me, for neither you nor any other creature could pick up that grain the way I have scattered it. Go tell *that* to your masters, Urisk!"

The Urisk swung its great head from side to side, looking at what he had done; then slowly it said, "You are not daft, right enough, MacAllister. But you are still not so clever as you think you are, for you have forgotten that the *sidhe* can take any shape they choose. And the birds of the air could pick up that grain as easy as you would sup porridge!"

With that, it turned and began running away over the hillside, letting out great bellowing cries as it ran. Like a dying bull it sounded, and MacAllister felt a shiver go up his back at the mournful noise echoing over the hill. He shook away the feeling, however, for although he realized the Urisk had spoken the truth, he was still determined not to let the *sidhe* steal his barley.

He stood pondering what he should do next, and Colm watched him, puzzled to know why he had let the Urisk go free when he had it trapped; for hunting the Urisk meant no more to Colm than hunting a deer. When Mac-

12

Allister made no move, he whined and pawed the ground where the Urisk had stood; and it was Colm scratching like this that gave MacAllister the idea he had been seeking.

Quickly he turned and rushed down the hill again, calling Colm with him. Back at his farm once more, he shut Colm in the barn, then snatched up a rake and went back up the hill at his best speed. Then, with great strong strokes, he began raking the ground where the barley lay all scattered among the grass and heather roots.

His rake bit deep, tearing right down to the bare earth. Heather and grass together came up with it, along with the barley trapped in their stems; and soon the purpose of his raking became clear, for every stroke he made helped to form this mixture of heather and grass and barley into a certain pattern. But making the pattern was a race against time. MacAllister had guessed that from the moment the Urisk gave its first mournful bellow, and he knew it for certain when another sound reached him faintly on the wind.

It was a wild, shrill chirruping of small birds he could hear, and glancing up he saw a great flock of them gathering like a cloud in the sky over the peak of Ben MacDui. His pattern was almost complete, however. He put the last few strokes to it, then hefted his rake and ran for shelter in a clump of rowan and elder wood growing farther down the hill. Once hidden there he felt reason-

13

ably safe, for rowan wood and elder wood are two power-ful charms against the magic of the *sidhe;* and so taking heart again, he peered upward through the leaves to the great flock of birds swooping toward him.

There were thousands of them, and as they came nearer and nearer the sound of their chirruping grew louder and wilder until it was like a scream trailing across the sky. The flock made the shape of a great blunt arrowhead that circled once over the spot where the grain had been spilled, and then shot straight down toward it.

Not one of these many birds touched the ground, however, for the leaders of the flock checked their flight while they were still well above the pattern MacAllister had made, and tried wildly to gain height again. The arrowhead broke into confusion. Birds wheeled, fluttered, and darted, and the air was frantic with the flurry of their wings and the sound of their screaming. Then slowly, from all this confusion, the flock reformed—and turned away for the flight back to Ben MacDui!

MacAllister watched them go, holding his breath for fear they would return for another attempt to pick up the grain. But even if they had done so, he knew they would not succeed the second time either, because the shape he had formed from all that grass and heather and barley raked together was the shape of a Christian cross. And for all their dark magic, that is the one thing in the world the *sidhe* dare not touch.

They were not finished with him yet, of course, for the

sidhe will never rest until they are revenged on anyone who has outwitted them. MacAllister knew that very well, but neither was he finished with the *sidhe*, because he was still determined not to give in to them over the Goodman's Croft. When the birds had finally disappeared, therefore, he went back down the hill a very thoughtful man, and the upshot of this thinking was the same as it had been over the two bags of barley.

"If I cannot get the use of the land," he decided, "then neither will the *sidhe*." And to this end, he immediately began setting shoots of rowan and elder in a hedge around the Goodman's Croft.

When this hedge was finally planted, he walked three times around it in a sunwise direction—that is, making a circle from left to right, taking care to tread exactly in his own footsteps each time; which is another powerful charm against the *sidhe*, and so there was now a double barrier between them and the Goodman's Croft.

MacAllister's neighbors came to watch him at this work, for some of them had seen the Urisk running away with the barley, and the great flock of birds that came over from Ben MacDui. Now they were curious to know the meaning of it all, and they gathered about the Goodman's Croft, calling questions to MacAllister as he tramped sunwise around it.

MacAllister smiled as he listened to them, for it struck him then that he had discovered a good way to get back into favor with Peigi-Ann. She would be just as curious as anyone else to discover how he had outwitted the *sidhe*, he decided; but he would keep that a secret from everyone, and so she would be sure to send for him so that she could try to wheedle it out of him!

"I am just making sure that what is mine will stay mine," he told the neighbors who asked him the reason for the rowan and elder hedge and the sunwise tramping. And to those who asked about the Urisk, he said,

"Oh, aye, the creature tried to rob me, sure enough, but I slashed the bags of barley with my dirk, and *that* put an end to his thieving for the *sidhe*."

"You had better stop calling them by their true name, MacAllister," one man said nervously, but MacAllister laughed.

"Why should I?" he asked. "I have outwitted them once. I can do it again if need be."

"How did you outwit them? What happened to the barley?" his neighbors asked; and so MacAllister told them how the Urisk had called up the *sidhe* in the shape of birds, but not a word would he say of what he had done to stop them picking up the barley. Try as they would, his neighbors could not get this out of him, but the Skeelie Woman was sharper than the rest, and she said,

"You cannot always keep it secret, MacAllister, for come next spring, the barley you spilled on the ground will grow again, and then your secret will be plain on the hillside for all to see."

16

"True," MacAllister agreed, enjoying himself. "And then it will be plain for *you* to see, too, that I was right when I said no Christian man need fear the old magic."

The Skeelie Woman fixed him with her strange eyes. "See that you remember that well, then," she said, "for you will need all the Christian grace you can find to set against the dark force of magic you have stirred up now, MacAllister."

Away she went in a flash of bright color and silver earrings, but MacAllister's mind was too full of Peigi-Ann to let this warning bother him. And as it happened, he had been right when he guessed that Peigi-Ann would not be able to resist the thought of a secret, for it was not long before she sent for him.

"Will you marry me if I tell you?" he asked when she tried to wheedle him into saying how he had outwitted the *sidhe*.

"I will not," said she, but she smiled and went on talking pleasantly all the same; and after a while she said she would not mind if MacAllister came courting again.

MacAllister guessed, of course, that she was just saying this so that she could keep trying to coax his secret out of him. But, he decided, half a loaf is better than no bread; and so, never dreaming that this would be the very thing to give the *sidhe* their chance to be revenged on him, he prepared to go courting his Peigi-Ann again.

2

THE GLOOMY PASS

MacAllister had a good distance to travel to Peigi-Ann's home—five or six hours riding altogether, in fact—for the track to it was by way of a *lairig,* as they call a mountain pass, and this *lairig* was a long one that cut right through the Cairngorm Mountains. The *Lairig Ghru*—the Gloomy Pass—it is called, for it is a wild and desolate place and even in high summer there are stretches of it that never see the sun.

It takes a bold man, therefore, to travel the Lairig Ghru at the best of times, and only a fool or a desperate man would do so in the bleak winter days when the snow winds come hurtling and shrieking down from the great mountains closing it in on either side. But MacAllister, of course, was a man in love, which meant that he cared nothing for the hardship and danger of the journey as long as he could see his Peigi-Ann at the end of it.

As often as he could that winter, therefore, he made this journey through the Lairig Ghru, leaving home early in the day to arrive before darkness fell, and setting out again early in the morning of the next day, since Peigi-Ann's parents would not hear of him traveling back through the pass in darkness.

This meant that he had to hire a man to look after his farm while he was away, and to do this he chose a fellow by the name of Murdo Mathieson—a decent sort of man who was strong in the arm although he was a bit short of sense. As sometimes happens with such simpleminded creatures, however, Murdo had a way with beasts, and so Colm was happy with him and MacAllister knew he had left his stock in good hands.

Peigi-Ann herself was pleased with such arrangements, since she thought they would give her all the more time to wheedle MacAllister's secret out of him—although MacAllister, of course, had no intention of loosing the hold this curiosity gave him over her. Yet even though he kept his mouth firmly shut about the cross on the hill he had plenty to say otherwise, for love had made quite a poet out of him.

Peigi-Ann was quite charmed by all the sweet talk he gave her, and wondering why she had ever driven him away from her at all, she soon began to welcome him for himself alone. And so, for a time at least that winter,

MacAllister's courting went very well.

Then there came a day early in the month of January when a fearful storm of wind blew up suddenly and carried away part of the roof of his barn. MacAllister had planned to start off on a visit to Peigi-Ann that day, but all the winter feed for his cattle was stored in that barn and he could not risk losing it to the gale. He called Murdo to help him; but hard as the two of them worked, the day-light was almost gone before they had the roof sound again, and MacAllister realized that he would have to ride the Lairig Ghru in darkness.

Yet so lost in love was he by this time that even this prospect could not daunt him, and so he saddled up as usual for the journey. Murdo watched him in dismay, and protested at last,

"You'll freeze in this bitter wind, MacAllister—both you and your beast!"

"Not a bit of it, Murdo," MacAllister told him cheer-fully, for with his bonnet pulled well down on his head and his plaid wrapped snugly round his shoulders, he was quite sure he could weather the worst the storm could do to him.

Murdo was not satisfied. "The Lairig Ghru is a terrible place all the same," he said gloomily. "Heaven alone knows what you might meet with there on a night like this."

"Well," returned MacAllister, "if Heaven knows, then

surely Heaven will protect me. So don't you be worrying, Murdo man." And off he set, with his mind fixed on Peigi-Ann and his spirits high.

The wind was fierce in his face as he turned it toward the Lairig Ghru, but there was a good track for the first hour or so of the journey and so it was fair progress he made to begin with. Then the track began to climb steeply toward the highest point of the pass, and the higher the track climbed, the rougher it became. The higher the track climbed also, the wilder blew the wind, and now there was snow as sharp and hard as shattered ice hurtling down with it.

MacAllister struggled on, however, trusting in his own youth and strength and the courage of the stout beast under him, but it took him twice as long as it usually did to reach the head of the pass. Once there, he began the long journey down the other side with a fold of his plaid pulled up over his mouth so that he could breathe without choking on the frozen blast that funneled up the narrow defile ahead, but there was nothing else he could do to protect himself from it.

His bonnet was snatched off by one fierce gust of wind, and went flying goodness knows where in the darkness. His face was stung raw and tender by the blatter of icy snow. His legs began to grow numb with cold, and his hands froze in their grip on the reins. He would have to find shelter soon, he realized, or poor Murdo would be proved right and he would indeed perish in this storm!

He peered ahead for a sight of the great cone-shaped mountain called The Devil's Peak, but darkness and whirling snow were all that met his eye. He could see the River Dee, however, rushing along on his right hand, and knew he must soon come to a fording place that led across the Dee to the foot of The Devil's Peak. He would find shelter then, he told himself, thinking of the cattle drovers' hut that stood on the far side of the ford.

Grimly he urged his horse on, telling himself that even a night in a drovers' bothy would be better than freezing to death like this; and as if it sensed there was shelter ahead for it also, the poor beast made one last effort for him.

MacAllister rode with his head inclined to the right so that he could watch out for the fording place across the River Dee, and it was only when he drew level with this ford that he looked beyond the river to The Devil's Peak itself. To his astonishment, then, he glimpsed a little star of yellow light shining against the black bulk of the mountain, and drew rein abruptly to stare at it.

It was coming from the little hut—the drovers' bothy—he realized. Indeed, there was no other place it could come from—which meant, surely, that some other traveler had already taken shelter there, and so he would at least have company while he waited out the storm!

The thought lifted his spirits so that he urged his horse across the river without any further pause to wonder at his good fortune. Eagerly then, he made for the dark outline of the bothy with its wonderful, welcoming gleam of light; and quickly dismounting there, he led his horse to the shelter of the small stable that leaned against one gable wall of the building.

He could hear voices coming from inside the bothy even while he did this, and he smiled as he slapped away the snow that had gathered on his shoulders. Then he made for the door of the bothy, and with his smile growing broader as his hand touched the latch, he pushed the door open.

A breath of warm air blew on his frozen face, and with pleasure he saw that there was a great fire blazing on the hearth of the bothy's one room. Nor were there only one or two travelers there, but a whole company of them—women as well as men. Their faces were turned toward him, their voices welcomed him in; then he was stepping over the threshold and making for the fire with his hands held gratefully out to the blaze.

The company made room for him, exclaiming at the state he was in, asking how far he had come, where he was bound, and other friendly questions. MacAllister could not have been made more welcome supposing he had been one of themselves, and in no time at all he found he was telling the whole story of the reason for his journey through the Lairig Ghru and why he had ventured out on such a night.

One of the ladies seated by the fire smiled when he

spoke of Peigi-Ann, and teasingly she said, "Your Peigi-Ann must be very beautiful to persuade you to make such a journey!"

She had a clarsach—a little harp—resting on her knee, and she was fingering its strings softly as she spoke. Mac-Allister glanced at it, and saw that the frame was made of gold, and the lady herself was very beautiful. She was also richly dressed, he noticed then, with golden combs in her hair, a gown made of silk, and shoes of finest, softest leather gleaming on her little feet. He glanced quickly at the rest of the company, and saw that they could all stand comparison with her.

They were young, all of them. The ladies were beautiful, the men were handsome, and they all wore the same kind of fine clothes made of silk, with ornaments of gold, and shoes of fine, soft leather. Indeed, MacAllister thought, he had never seen a company so elegant; but being a man with a proper pride in his own worth, he did not let this dismay him. Nor was he at a loss for an answer to the young woman with the clarsach.

"My Peigi-Ann *is* beautiful, mistress," he told her. "She is as beautiful as yourself."

Everyone laughed and applauded this remark. Mac-Allister was nicely thawed out by this time, and he joined in the laughter. He felt a friendly touch on his shoulder, and one of the young men turned him about to face the other end of the room, where there was a table laid out with food and drink.

24

"You see," said the young man, "we have come prepared for our journey, and you must join us in our meal."

"Gladly!" MacAllister answered. And smiling, blessing his luck in having fallen in with such pleasant company, he let himself be led toward the table.

The young woman with the clarsach struck another, louder, chord from it. A few of the company began singing to the quick, rippling tune it signaled. Some of them danced to the music, and others crowded toward the table. MacAllister found himself caught up in all this gaiety, with someone pushing a glass of wine into his hand and someone else heaping a plateful of cold roast chicken for him.

The lady with the little harp smiled at him, and MacAllister thought he had never seen a smile so sweet or heard music so enchanting. The dancers called gaily to him, and he stood amazed at the grace and lightness of their movements. He bowed to the lady with the harp, raising his glass of wine to her. He smiled to the dancers, glancing again at their light, swift feet, and was about to put his glass to his lips when he realized something that made him hesitate.

There was not a speck of dirt or damp on a single foot of all that company!

And yet, MacAllister thought, they had spoken as if they were travelers who had ridden through the same storm that had driven him for shelter! But if that was so, where were their horses? There had not been even one other beast in the lean-to where he had left his own horse!

MacAllister put his glass down on the table, feeling his blood suddenly run cold. If these people were not travelers, then who were they? The clarsach was still playing, but the music seemed to ring in his ears now with an unearthly sweetness. The dancers were still moving, but now it seemed to him there was something uncanny in the way their feet fell light as feathers on the rough floor of the bothy. Their silken clothes and golden ornaments were flashing in the light—but where did that light come from? There were no candles or lamps in the room that he could see.

"Come, drink up!" a voice said cheerfully at his elbow, and MacAllister turned to the young man who had spoken. Was it imagination, he wondered, or had he seen a gleam of triumph on that handsome face? He thought of the cross on the hill above his farm, and the revenge the *sidhe* were bound to seek for it. He saw that the young man and his friends were the height of normal people, but remembered that the *sidhe* could take any form they chose; then reached for his glass with a hand that had begun to shake a little.

If what he suspected was true, he thought, and these beautiful strangers really were a company of the *sidhe*, there was only one way to save himself from them. He looked the young man in the eye again, and said bluntly,

"You have forgotten something, have you not? You have not said the grace before meat."

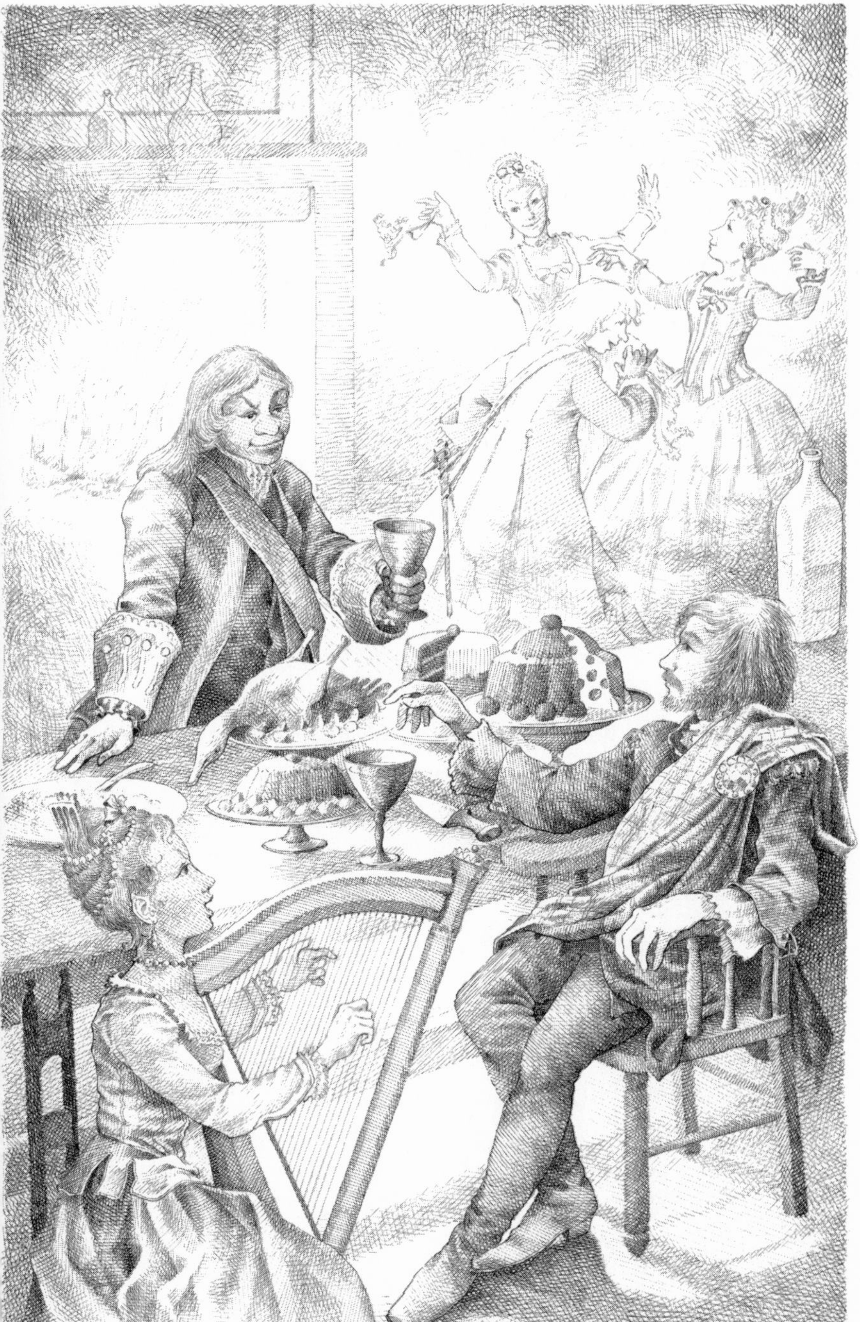

The young man's smiling face grew suddenly still. He bit his lip, staring at MacAllister; then trying to force the smile again, he cried,

"Ach, there is no need to be so solemn! Drink up, man, and enjoy yourself!"

"Not yet," MacAllister answered stubbornly, "for I am accustomed always to ask a blessing before a drop or a bite touches my lips." Then trying hard to keep the tone of his voice steady, he bowed his head over the wine and said, "Bless this food and drink to our use, O Lord, and ourselves to Thy service."

On the instant that he spoke, MacAllister heard the music of the clarsach rise to a wailing shriek that was wilder even than the shrieking of the storm outside. A great gust of cold wind rushed over him, rocking him on his feet. The shrieking grew louder . . . higher. . . . MacAllister was whirled around like a leaf by the cold wind, until it seemed to him that the wind and the shrieking were one and the same great force spinning him round and round.

Then suddenly he crashed against the table. His head hit the edge of it and he fell down, down, and down, with silence and darkness settling over him like a blanket being gently drawn over his head.

When MacAllister opened his eyes again, he had no idea of how long he had lain stunned on the bothy floor. Slowly and carefully he gripped the edge of the table,

28

and pulling himself to his feet, he looked around the bothy. He was alone there, now. The only dancers were the shadows cast by the flames of the fire still flickering on the hearth. There was no other light in the room, and reaching out a hand to the fire, MacAllister pulled a burning stick from it.

Those beautiful people with their fine clothes, he thought, had indeed been a company of the *sidhe*, and they had scattered in panic from the sound of a Christian blessing on their feast. But what would have happened to *him* if he had drunk their wine and eaten their food? With his stick held up like a torch he went over to the table and examined the meal set out on it.

The fine feast looked very different now, he saw with a shiver, for now the plates of food were only big dock leaves heaped high with poisonous toadstools. The knives and forks beside them were only twigs. The wineglasses were only acorn cups, and the stuff inside them gave off the poisonous smell of the deadly nightshade berry.

It was a feast of death the *sidhe* had prepared for him, MacAllister thought, and in a sudden burst of anger he heaved the table over. It fell with a crash, and in the stillness that followed MacAllister realized he could no longer hear the wind shrieking around the bothy.

He went to the door and peered into the quiet dark outside. There was a powdering of snow underfoot, and the black rocks of the pass were glittered with its icy crystals, but the storm seemed to have ended as suddenly as it had begun that day.

MacAllister looked at the traces it had left and wondered. Had the *sidhe* raised it, knowing he would defy it in order to see Peigi-Ann and then be forced to take shelter in the bothy? That was very likely the case, he thought, for how was it possible otherwise for it to begin and end so suddenly?

But if the *sidhe* had gone to the trouble of raising a storm to trap him into eating their death-feast, that was surely the measure of their spite against him—and so what was he to do now? Give in to them? Go home and tear out the elder and rowan wood guarding the Goodman's Croft? Admit defeat?

"Never!" MacAllister told himself, but now there was more in his mind than the stubborn desire to have his own way; and standing there alone among the snow-scattered rocks he argued the matter out to its conclusion.

Now, he thought, he knew the real difference between his own kind and the people of the *sidhe,* and so now he knew his real reason for refusing to give them the Goodman's Croft. The *sidhe* had power, beauty, wealth—everything the heart could desire; but they had no souls, and so they were still less than men.

He had nothing except his land—but it was working his own land, living by his own land, that gave him the right to call himself a man among men. And he would have no proper pride in himself again if he gave up the least part of that right to creatures that were less than men!

He would never, never yield so much as an inch of his land to the *sidhe*, MacAllister vowed. *"Never!"* He cried the word aloud, lifting his head to the lonely dark all around him, and the ghostly echo of his voice sent *". . . never . . . never . . . never . . ."* crying along the rocky wastes of the pass.

MacAllister let the sound die away, then cupped his hands to his mouth and shouted even louder. *"The land is mine!"* he shouted up to the mountains towering over the Lairig Ghru.

The small, human sound of his voice bounced against the great stone sides of the mountains, and was thrown back in a drum roll of echoes that boomed, *"MINE . . . MINE . . . MINE . . .!"* And standing there, with his feet in the powdered snow and his voice among the mountains, MacAllister had the strange feeling that one man had cried defiance at last for all men against the power of the *sidhe* and the fear of their strong and ancient magic.

There was still the rest of the night to be lived through, however, and still the rest of the pass to ride, for he could see no point in staying trapped in the bothy for the *sidhe* to have another try at him. As they were sure to do, Mac-Allister thought, knowing that they always came back and back again when they were thwarted in any purpose. And certainly they would never have a better chance for that purpose than this dark night in the Lairig Ghru!

3

THE WHITE MARE

MacAllister mounted his horse and forded the River Dee again, wondering just where and when the *sidhe* would strike at him, but he would have been wiser to keep his mind on the matter in hand for it is just at this point in the Lairig Ghru that it is possible to miss the way.

The track splits into two here, both parts of it running side by side for a mile or so and then the left-hand one bearing east through the remainder of the Lairig Ghru while the right-hand one runs south into Glen Dee. The snow hid this fork in the path from MacAllister; besides which, the malice of the *sidhe* was working against him. And so, without noticing what he was doing, he took the right-hand path into Glen Dee.

The air seemed strangely quiet after all the howling of the storm. MacAllister could hear nothing but the hoofbeats of his horse, and he found himself listening uneasily for some other sound as he rode along. It was still very dark too, in spite of the white glimmer of snow on the ground, and he could see nothing of the mountains all around him. He had a strong sense of their presence, however, vast and mysterious in the night, and it made him feel very lonely to think he was the one human creature among all these giant, stony shapes.

His thoughts grew very gloomy, and he searched the sky for some bright, hopeful star to keep him company; but the stars were only a pale and distant frosting on the sky's huge dark, and his loneliness grew terrible to bear.

Supposing he were to die here, alone in this dark and dreadful night, he asked himself. Would anyone ever discover what had happened to him? Would Peigi-Ann ever know what he had dared for her sake? Would she mourn for him?

The thought of Peigi-Ann weeping pierced his heart and even made him consider breaking his vow never to give in to the *sidhe*; but MacAllister was a man who would sooner suffer a broken heart than take a broken vow on his conscience, and so he fought this temptation with all his might. For some time also, his horse had been acting strangely, always trying to veer away to the left of the path, and he had to rouse himself from his gloomy thoughts at last when it looked as if he might lose control of the beast altogether.

34

It was at this point in his journey that MacAllister realized he had taken the wrong path, for he could see the broad stream of the River Dee still flowing on his right hand; whereas, if he had been in the Lairig Ghru, he would have had the much narrower stream of the Luibeg Burn on his right. He must be in Glen Dee, he thought in dismay; and his horse had been much wiser than himself in choosing its direction, for he would indeed have to veer to the left now to regain the Lairig Ghru!

He let the beast have its head then, and immediately as he did this it turned to strike off across the moor on the left of the path. It had gone no more than a few yards, however, when MacAllister saw a white shape looming up out of the darkness to his right. For a moment his heart nearly stopped in terror, then his horse whinnied. There came an answering whinny out of the gloom, and to his relief, MacAllister realized that the white shape was only another horse.

The creature came up to them and paced alongside for a few steps while it nuzzled his own horse in greeting. It had no saddle or bridle on it, MacAllister saw; but it was a sleek beast, well-groomed and full-fleshed, so that it was clearly not from a wild herd. It was a mare, he noted also, and with the keen eye of a man who knows horseflesh he surveyed her finely arched neck and long, delicate legs.

The white mare drew ahead, stepping in a most purposeful manner, and MacAllister's horse made to follow her. He let it do so, since the white mare's direction was the one he had been set on in any case; and following behind the pale glimmer of her coat he decided she must be a stray that had wandered in search of a sweeter bite than she could find in her home pasture.

Now, he thought, she was stepping so certainly that she must be on her way home again; and so it would surely not be long before he came to some house where he would find how much farther he had to ride to the Lairig Ghru, or else discover the right direction for it if he had missed his way.

So for a mile and then part of a mile MacAllister followed the white mare over the moorland, and although there was no path that he could see, she never faltered in her stride. The moor began to take an upward slope, and the going became rougher with the ground breaking up into ridges that had patches of bog between them. Fortunately, however, there was no snow to put a false crust on these boggy patches, for the storm that had hit the Lairig Ghru seemed to have missed this stretch of moorland.

MacAllister shrugged off his plaid, grateful for the warmer air, and found himself at last facing two tall hillocks with a broad stream tumbling down between them. The white mare made straight for these hillocks, and he followed her along the bank of the stream. A scent of

36

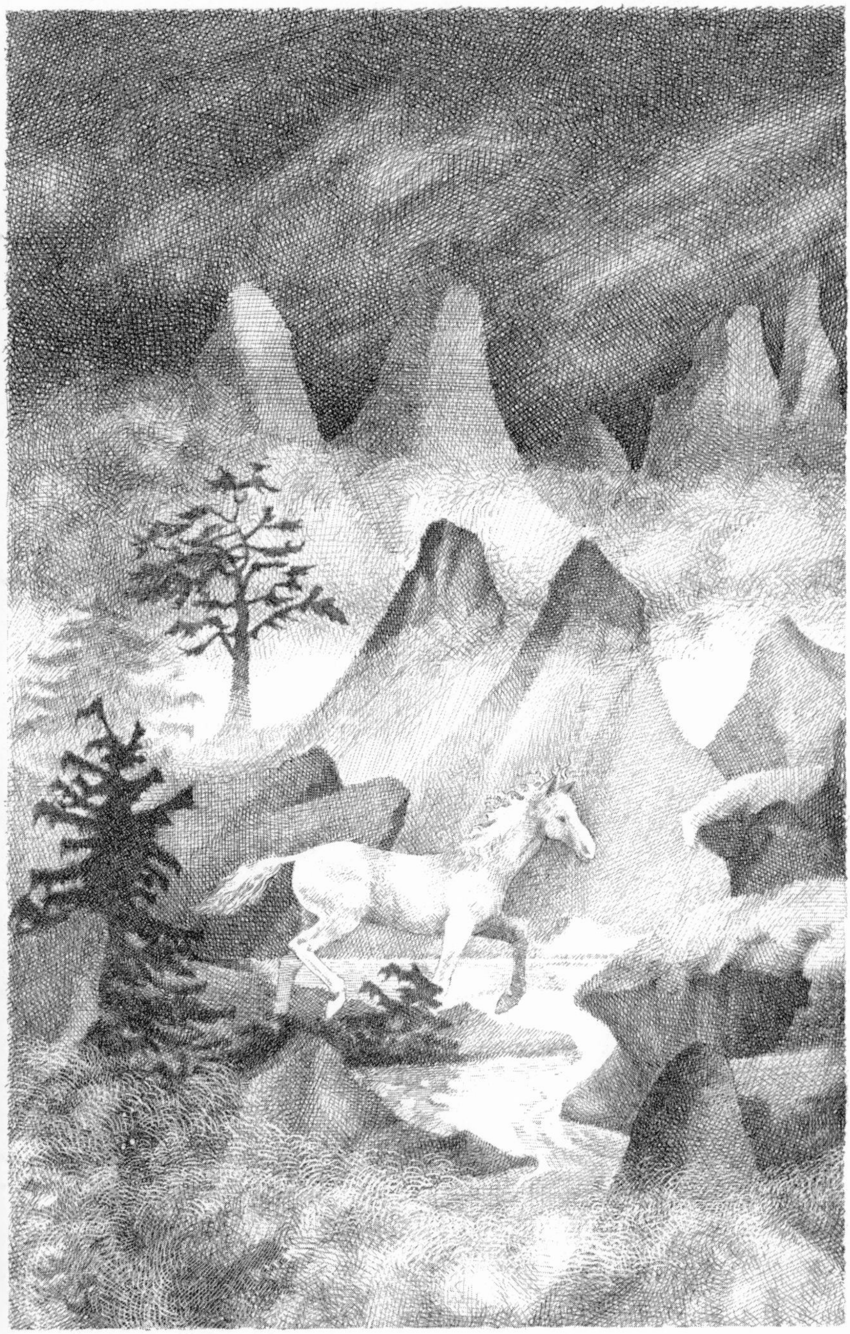

peat smoke reached him as he did so, and he sniffed it eagerly, telling himself that he had been nearer the mark than he thought when he guessed that the white mare was on her way home.

Somewhere not too far away, there must be a house that had its hearth fire banked for the night with the peats that were smelling so sweetly!

On the far side of the two hillocks there was a small meadow; then another hillock, and another, and another —in fact, MacAllister found, there was an absolute maze of hillocks with little streams wandering down among them and little meadows cupped like secrets between them. The white mare seemed quite familiar with this maze, however, for she still paced steadily on, making a winding way around the hillocks from one patch of meadow to the next.

She made so many twists and turns, indeed, that Mac-Allister gradually lost all sense of direction; and even though he could still smell the peat smoke, he wondered if she was going back on her tracks at some points. Then, as suddenly as she had first appeared, she vanished again. MacAllister came around the shoulder of one of the hillocks thinking she was just ahead of him, but when he reached the meadow beyond it there was no sign at all of the white mare.

Puzzled, and not a little put out at this, he sat staring at the meadow and the hillocks that cupped it. A breath

38

of cold wind touched his neck, and he shivered, pulling his plaid close around him again. There was a gray light growing in the sky now, and for the first time he noticed how strangely the gorse bushes on the hillocks were outlined against this grayness. The dry, twisted branches thrusting out from the grass were like withered arms upstretched, he thought; and the spiky twigs sticking out from the end of each branch were like the clawing fingers of bony hands!

He shivered again, although his plaid now lay warm around him; then, sharply telling himself not to be so fanciful, he urged his horse forward. It would catch the scent of the white mare, he thought, and so find it again; but his horse only walked to the center of the meadow and stood there with its head sadly drooping.

Clearly, MacAllister thought, it had no more idea of the white mare's whereabouts than he had himself—but that did not matter so much now, for now the smell of peat smoke was strong in his nostrils!

The house it came from *must* be near at hand, he told himself, and with another glance at the gray light in the sky, decided he would try to catch a glimpse of the house from the top of the high hillock beside him. Better that, he thought, than risk wandering farther through this maze without the white mare to guide him.

Riding to the foot of the hillock then, he dismounted, and left his horse to wait below while he climbed up the slope. The smell of peat smoke grew even stronger as he climbed, and when he was almost at the top of the hillock, he got a mouthful of it that nearly choked him. He went down on one knee, gasping for breath, and his right hand touched something warm in the grass.

It was the lip of a hole, he realized, a smooth, stone-lined hole; and it was from this hole that the smoke was drifting! He peered downward, but could see no blink of fire, and cautiously he felt farther and farther down the hole. His arm went in right up to the shoulder, bringing his ear down level with the hole, and immediately he heard voices drifting up to him. For a moment then, he lay absolutely still, his body frozen with shock although his mind was racing; for now he knew that the hole was a chimney shaft for a fire *inside* the hillock. And there could be only one reason for that!

This was a *sidhean*—the kind of dwelling the *sidhe* hollowed out for themselves from the hill and the ground beneath it. And very likely, his thoughts ran on, every one of those hillocks around him was a *sidhean* also. This maze must be the place of the hollow hills where the whole tribe of the *sidhe* were said to dwell, and the white mare had been a decoy to lead him to it!

Inch by inch MacAllister withdrew his arm, listening all the time to the ghostly sound of the voices drifting up to him, and with a further shock of alarm he heard his own name mentioned. A burst of laughter followed, and another confused babble of voices. Then one that was louder than the rest cried out,

"But soon MacAllister will be ours to do with as we choose, for he will not be able to speak his Christian prayers once he is trapped in the place of hollow hills!"

MacAllister felt panic gripping him at this. He tried to pray, and found the words all jumbled like nonsense in his mind. It was true, he thought wildly. The *sidhe* were all-powerful in their own territory!

For a moment then, he almost gave up hope, but the thought of his Peigi-Ann waiting for him would not let him despair. Moreover, he was naturally too stubborn to admit himself beaten by even this kind of situation. There must be *some* way out of the maze of hillocks, he told himself, and if only he could find it he would be able to fight the *sidhe* on his own terms again.

He thought hard, and suddenly remembered the broad stream at the entrance to the maze. *That* was the answer, he told himself. All the little streams between the hillocks must run down to join that one broad stream at last, and so all he had to do was to follow any one of them until it did so. But he would have to start right away, before the white mare's return to this place betrayed his presence in it!

Quickly and quietly he went down the hillock, then swung into the saddle and guided his horse toward the stream that flowed on the far side of the meadow. He put it to the gallop along the bank of the stream, thinking

41

to himself that the noise the creature made would soon be heard in the underground kingdom of the *sidhe*; but at least he would give them a run for their money! And when the pursuit grew too hot . . .

MacAllister left this thought to take care of itself and put his mind to the business in hand, for the stream he had chosen was as twisted as all the others running through the maze. It wandered slowly through a meadow here, ran fast between hillocks there. Its banks were boggy in some places, stony in others, and following it through the network of other streams that met it was like trying to hold on to a single thread in a great, tangled skein.

MacAllister cut as many corners as he could, jumping his horse over pools and bends wherever he dared; but the winding way soon slowed his first galloping pace. And as the minutes slipped by, he began to have the desperate feeling of a man who tries to run from the terror of a nightmare, only to find he has lead weights on his feet.

His horse began to labor with the effort of all the jumping and scrambling he was forcing on it; but Mac-Allister urged it on, listening all the time for sounds of pursuit to reach him over the noise it was making. A rocky outcrop barred his way. He scrambled his horse up it and jumped it blindly down the other side. The bank of the stream gave way to bog—and now he *could* faintly hear the *sidhe* pursuing him! There was a sound of screaming in the air—a high, thin sound that rose into a wild wailing, and fell again to a whine like that of angry bees.

Desperately he jumped his horse over the stream to try the other bank, and found it just as boggy. His beast sank fetlock-deep into the black peat mud. It struggled clear, but there was panic in it now. MacAllister could see that in the way its ears were laid close to its head. He could feel it in the sweat starting out on its neck. And every second, the sounds of pursuit were drawing nearer!

It was time to try to throw the *sidhe* off his trail, he decided; and since they had only the sound of his horse's hoofbeats to guide them, he knew what he had to do. He waited for the next stretch of meadow to appear, and when it opened out on his left, he swung his horse sharply in that direction. The creature burst into a gallop again, just as he had expected it would when it felt firm ground and saw open space ahead; and easing his feet from the stirrups, MacAllister threw himself headlong from the saddle.

As he struck the ground and rolled over, he caught one last glimpse of his horse still galloping on in the grip of its panic. Then it was gone, and he was pulling himself to his feet again. The fall had knocked him breathless, but that was all the harm it had done, and back he ran to the stream. Swift and silent he sped on down its bank, and had only run for a few moments when he heard the sounds of pursuit behind him veer off to follow the noise of his horse's galloping.

"So you still have a chance, MacAllister!" he told himself grimly, and ran on until he felt that his heart would break and his lungs burst with the sheer effort of it. Yet still he ran, and better ran, and saw this chance become a firm hope at last as the little stream beside him tumbled into a wide, brawling one with a tall hillock on either side of it.

Like the winner of a race making his last spurt for the finishing post then, MacAllister ran toward the hillocks and burst triumphantly through the gap between them. Before him lay the moor over which he had followed the white mare. To his right, the shoulder of Ben MacDui stood black against the dawn sky. He stared at the mountain, still hardly able to believe that he had escaped at last from the place of the hollow hills.

He blinked, and stared again. The moor was still there, and so was the mountain. He really had escaped, he assured himself, and the *sidhe* were not all-powerful outside their own territory. Let them pursue him beyond this point if they wished, he was not afraid of them now!

MacAllister turned his face toward the Lairig Ghru then, and set off at a good pace on the last of his journey to Peigi-Ann's home. Fast as he walked, however, it was not fast enough to please him, and he could not help wishing he still had his horse to shorten the journey. He had to smile, all the same, when he thought of the *sidhe* chasing the riderless beast in the belief that they were chasing him also!

A horse—even a good riding beast—was a small price

to pay for his life, he told himself cheerfully; and at least the *sidhe* would have *some* return for this second trick he had played on them!

His smile became a grin, the grin became a chuckle, and the dawn light beginning to sparkle on the snowcaps of the mountains ahead sent his spirits soaring still higher. He laughed out loud, and suddenly found he could no longer contain his thoughts of Peigi-Ann in silence; for a man who has just escaped with his life is not a reasonable being, while a man in love who has just made such an escape is little better than a madman.

"*Peigi-Ann! Peigi-Ann!*" MacAllister cried then to the rose-colored sparkle of snow on the mountaintops, and thought he had never heard sweeter music than the sound of that name.

"*Peigi-Ann! Peigi-Ann!*" he shouted to the gold and indigo and green of sunrise streaking the sky behind the great black bulk of Ben MacDui.

"*Peigi-Ann! Peigi-Ann!*" he called to the cloud banners flying purple and scarlet and flamingo pink above The Devil's Peak.

"*Peigi-Ann! Peigi-Ann! Peigi-Ann!*" MacAllister sang the name of his love to all the jewel colors glowing above and between and around the snowcapped mountains glittering in that dawn; and the glory of these mad moments was still on his face when he came in sight of Peigi-Ann's house at last and saw her come running to meet him.

45

MacAllister stared at her red-gold hair shining in the glow of the risen sun, and wondered at the flame of it. He gazed down at her flower-pale face, and thought no flower could be more perfect. He looked long into the blue of her eyes, and feeling that his heart would break for the deep, dark beauty of them, he said humbly,

"Peigi-Ann, will you marry me?"

Peigi-Ann looked up at this handsome young man towering dark and strong over her. She sensed the fire of triumph and pride that was in him, and guessed he had come to her out of some great trouble. She saw the glory in his face, and knew it was his love for her that had given him the strength to defeat that trouble. Her own heart caught fire suddenly from the fire that raged in his, and she answered,

"I will, oh, I will! Yes, I will marry you!"

4

THE HAPPY YEARS . . .

MacAllister never again traveled the Lairig Ghru in darkness, and he kept to himself all the things that had happened on the night of the storm. However, he did tell Peigi-Ann about the cross he had made from the barley spilled on the hillside, and this calmed her fears of the *sidhe*. She quickly set a date for the wedding, and MacAllister began to make certain preparations of his own for it.

The first thing he did was to nail a horseshoe above the door of his house; then he nailed one above the door of his barn and another one above the door of his byre. For good measure also, he fixed a branch of rowan wood above each door; then he got some red thread and tied a length of it around the horns of every cow he possessed. Last of all he took some silver coins and dropped one into every bucket and trough used for his animals' drinking water, then nailed the coins into position there.

Murdo Mathieson, the hired man, was quite bewildered by all this activity, but he kept his tongue between his teeth until MacAllister came to perform "the silvering of the water," as they call it. This was altogether too much for Murdo's curiosity, and he asked then,

"What way do you need to do all this, MacAllister, before you bring a woman into the house?"

"Well, Murdo," MacAllister explained, "here is the truth of it. The *sidhe* have been trying to get their spite out on me over the Goodman's Croft, but they have not been able to harm me thus far and so they might try to strike at me through Peigi-Ann, or even through my beasts. However, they cannot steal a beast that has the red thread for a charm around its horns, nor can they make it sicken if it drinks only the silvered water. And they certainly cannot come into any place that is protected by rowan wood or a horseshoe."

"I believe you," said Murdo. "But what will Peigi-Ann think of all this?"

"We'll see when the time comes," MacAllister told him, and went on to attend to other matters—such as his new coat for the wedding.

It was in the month of April this took place, Peigi-Ann having decided she wanted to be a spring bride. Half the Highlands came to the celebrations, which lasted for three days and were voted the best wedding the North had ever seen. Peigi-Ann's parents saw her off in style, then, with all those that were still fit to sit a horse riding escort with her and MacAllister back to his own house. And so Peigi-Ann came in sight of her new home at last.

The first thing her eyes lighted on there was the shape of a great green cross on the ground of the hill above the house, for the barley MacAllister had raked into this shape had sprouted and was growing well by this time. She pulled in her horse and sat for a good few moments staring at the great cross shining in the sunlight; then she turned to MacAllister and said gravely,

"That will be a fine view to have from the window of my new home."

"There is more yet to see," MacAllister told her, and waited to hear what she would say about the rowan wood and red thread and the horseshoe over each door. Peigi-Ann never mentioned these, however, until the last guest had left them together under their own roof; but then she spoke her mind clearly.

"If I still have something to fear from the *sidhe*," she told MacAllister, "I want to know what it is."

"Aye, well," MacAllister agreed. "You have a right to know, I suppose," and went straight on from there to tell her the full story of the death-feast the *sidhe* had prepared for him and the white mare they had sent to decoy him into the place of hollow hills.

49

Peigi-Ann was horrified by all this, yet still she could not help being proud of MacAllister for the courage and cunning that had brought him safely through these dangers. She told him so at the end of his story; then she said,

"And if you say the *sidhe* cannot pass all these charms now, I believe that we are both safe here. But why do you trouble to fight them like this? Why can you not just give them back the Goodman's Croft and be done with it?"

"Never!" said MacAllister. "I will never do that."

"Not even for me?" Peigi-Ann coaxed.

"Not even for you," MacAllister insisted.

"Och, you are stubborn!" Peigi-Ann exclaimed. Her lip quivered, and to hide the tears that threatened, she went outside to talk to Murdo.

"There is more to it than being stubborn," MacAllister called after her. Then he followed her outside and said earnestly, "There is something you must try to understand, Peigi-Ann. The land is my life, and no one is going to take part of my life from me, or I will be no proper man. Is that what you want for a husband?"

Peigi-Ann turned and measured him with a long look from the depth of her blue eyes. She was not sure if she understood this reasoning of his, but he looked so handsome in his velvet wedding coat with the silver buttons down the front that she could not be angry with him.

"I want the man I have," she told him. And so the matter was closed between them.

MacAllister's neighbors still whispered of it, however;

for now that they had seen the cross on the hill they could see, too, that a man need not always lose a battle against the *sidhe*. More than one of them began to resent the presence of the Goodman's Croft on his own farm, yet still none of them dared hedge it with rowan and elder as MacAllister had done. The fear of the *sidhe* was still too strong on them for that, and in their whisperings about MacAllister, there was much dark wondering on the price he might yet have to pay for his defiance.

MacAllister himself was not troubled by such thoughts, for he had long since decided that if he could survive the night of storm in the Lairig Ghru, he could survive anything the *sidhe* might bring against him. Peigi-Ann was soon won around to the same view, and with the great love and tenderness there was between them they were as happy as two people could be.

MacAllister worked hard on his farm—although he still found time to go hunting with Colm—and with Murdo to help him the land prospered. Peigi-Ann looked after the hens and the ducks and the geese. She was kind to poor, simple Murdo. She carded and spun the wool from the few sheep they had. She treated Colm with a proper respect for his dignity as a hunting dog, and so won as much obedience from him as An Cu Mor gave to MacAllister himself. She baked and she brewed, and if she fed MacAllister like a king, she was a queen in her own household.

"I have the best wife in the land," MacAllister told

everyone proudly, and for all that other men might smile behind their hands at such foolishness, he did not care.

Peigi-Ann smiled at this too, but only because she was so happy. Yet that was not the end of it, for when they had been married a year and a half she had a son with dark hair and dark eyes like his father's; and if MacAllister had been proud before there was no holding him then!

"We will call him Fergus," he declared, looking into the cradle, for "Fergus" means "strong" and the baby was certainly a sturdy one. MacAllister and Peigi-Ann doted on him, although he looked ordinary enough to every other eye, and Colm took to him from the start.

A year passed, and Fergus learned to walk. Another year passed, and he was running about outside in all weathers, following his father at the plow, chattering nonsense to Murdo, and tumbling about on the grass with Colm. MacAllister and Peigi-Ann watched him grow, and thought that the sun only rose to shine on their Fergus; and every day saw them more content with their life and with one another.

By the time Fergus was four, however, he had taken to wandering too far afield for Peigi-Ann to keep a proper eye on him. Yet even so, she had no cause to worry, for Colm went everywhere with him and was always on hand to pull him back to dry land if he tumbled into a burn, or to guard him against the occasional wildcat they disturbed among the rocky places of the hillside.

"An Cu Mor has turned nurse," people said, smiling at the thought. And of course it was comical in a way to see this big, dignified hunting dog trotting at the heels of a little boy who hardly reached to his shoulder. Yet there were some people who found nothing comical at all about it. These people looked at the great strength in Colm's lean muscles. They saw the sharpness of his long white teeth, and occasionally one of them would say to MacAllister,

"Are you not afraid to trust a small, helpless child to that huge beast?"

This always made MacAllister angry. "Afraid!" he would snort. "That hound is wise for speech, I tell you, and it's you should be afraid to say such a thing in his hearing. Colm would give his life for that boy!"

The dark-eyed little Skeelie Woman was present on one occasion when MacAllister said this and she gave him one of her strange looks. MacAllister paid small attention to this, however, being still concerned with his argument; but the Skeelie Woman followed him when he turned away, and with a hand on his arm to stop him she said,

"You maybe spoke truer than you know, MacAllister, when you said that Colm would give his life for the boy."

"Supposing I did," returned MacAllister, suspicious of the way she was eyeing him. "What is that to you, Skeelie Woman?"

"Nothing," said she, "except what you choose to give me for reading the future for you."

MacAllister was silent, remembering how truly she had warned him that he had much to fear from the magic of the *sidhe*. Then he remembered also how soundly he had defeated that magic, for Fergus was almost five years old by this time, which made it well over six years since he had first defied the *sidhe*. And, he thought, if the charms of rowan tree and red thread had protected himself and his family all that time, there was no reason why they should not protect them forever.

"I do not need you to read the future of my Fergus," he told the Skeelie Woman, but she only eyed him more cunningly than ever, and said,

"I was not talking about Fergus only, MacAllister, but of yourself as well; and if you meet my price, I will say more."

MacAllister looked from the silver buckles on her shoes to the silver rings in her ears, and thought there were few women in the glen who could afford such ornaments. "You make enough as it is," said he, "from those who are silly enough to pay for the clatter of your tongue. But *I* am not afraid of the day I never saw, and I am man enough to take care of my wife and child as well as myself. And so good-day to you, Skeelie Woman."

The Skeelie Woman bore him no malice for this speech. "The clatter of my tongue, as you call it, will be needed yet," she told him. "Tell your wife that, MacAllister, for she is not so stubborn as you are. And so good-day to you too, and may you never have to prove your words."

On that last warning word from her they parted, and although MacAllister was not unduly worried by their conversation he did tell Peigi-Ann about it, for he had come to have great respect for her good sense. Peigi-Ann thought about the matter, but like MacAllister himself she just could not believe that the future would be any less happy for them than the past had been.

"Think no more of it," she advised. "We have more to do with our gear than waste it on fortune-telling."

This chimed so exactly with MacAllister's own views that he thought it sound advice. Also, it was harvesttime, which meant they were all much too busy to sit around brooding on what only might happen. MacAllister therefore got on with the work of harvesting his crops, and soon forgot all about his conversation with the Skeelie Woman. Murdo and Peigi-Ann helped with the harvest, and even Fergus took a hand in it, being big enough that year to fetch and carry for them all.

When the harvest was all in, Murdo and MacAllister cut great cartloads of peat for their winter fires, and then it was time to think about a birthday present for Fergus, who would be five years old on the 7th of November that year. Peigi-Ann had saved a little money toward this, and MacAllister still had some of his summer wool clip to sell. They discussed what they should buy with Peigi-Ann's savings and the money they would get for the wool, and at the end of October Peigi-Ann said,

"If you could ride to the town and buy me a length of velvet, I would make Fergus a coat of it—with silver buttons down the front! That would be a brave present!"

"Aye, he would like that," MacAllister agreed, for he knew how much Fergus envied him his own wedding coat with the silver buttons down the front.

So it was decided, and MacAllister rode off to town with Peigi-Ann's few shillings in his pouch and the bundle of sheep's wool before him on the saddle. Peigi-Ann got out her scissors and needles and thread, all ready to start sewing the minute she got her hands on the velvet, and waited impatiently for MacAllister to return home.

Night came without any glimpse of him, and Peigi-Ann lit the lamps. All night she waited, and by the morning the lamps were burned out but still there was no sign of MacAllister. All the next day she waited, and all the next night, yet still he had not returned. With her sleepless eyes red from weeping then, Peigi-Ann went out to ask her neighbors for help, and the men of the glen formed a search party to look for MacAllister.

They rode to town and found he had bought the velvet there, and so it was on the way home that he must have come to grief—if he had come to grief. They searched all around the track back to the glen therefore, and found the bundle of velvet lying beside a stream not far from the track, but there was no further trace there of MacAllister or his horse.

For three days more they searched, uphill and downhill, farther and farther afield each time, but still had to admit the bitter truth in the end. MacAllister, it seemed, had vanished; and if some disaster had overtaken him, his body was nowhere to be found.

"You will have to face up to it, mistress. He must be dead," they told Peigi-Ann, and the women who had gathered in her house to wait for their return burst into tears and lamentations.

Fergus bawled and wept along with them, although he was too young to understand what he was weeping for, but

57

Peigi-Ann's tears were all finished now. She thanked the men and sat with a face like stone while the women fussed around her and comforted the crying of Fergus. Then, when Fergus had fallen asleep and the last of the sorrowful women had taken leave of her, she rose and took her shawl from its hook on the door. Colm also rose to his feet, all ready to follow her, but she told him,

"No, Colm. Stay and guard the boy."

The great hound turned obediently to stretch himself at the foot of the bed where Fergus lay sleeping, and putting her shawl over her head, Peigi-Ann went up the glen to see the Skeelie Woman.

5

...AND THE SAD ONES

"I have little to give," Peigi-Ann told the Skeelie Woman, "but you may have it all if you can tell me what has happened to my husband."

The Skeelie Woman looked at her with pity. "A body must live," she said, "but I am not so grasping as you think, Peigi-Ann, and I am sorry for you. I will see what I can see and let payment take care of itself for the moment."

With that she rose and fetched a large silver spoon. She gave this spoon to Peigi-Ann to hold, then she took a jar of some stuff that looked like black ink and poured out enough of this to fill the bowl of the spoon.

"Now cup the bowl of the spoon in your left hand," she told Peigi-Ann, "and hold it to the light."

Peigi-Ann cupped the bowl of the spoon as she was told,

holding it to the light of the one candle in the room, and the candlelight made a little spot of gold on the dark stuff that filled the spoon. The Skeelie Woman stared at this spot of golden light, and as she stared, it seemed to Peigi-Ann that the spot increased in size and grew paler; and widened yet, growing paler all the time until it seemed it was not a spoon she held but a handful of clear light.

"You may not like what I see here," the Skeelie Woman warned as she stared into this little lit pool, but Peigi-Ann told her harshly,

"Like it or not, Skeelie Woman, I must know the truth."

"Then listen," said she, "for now I can see MacAllister riding home from the town. There is an old woman—a poor, weary scarecrow of a creature—resting beside the track. I see her greet MacAllister, and ask him for a *culag.*"

Now a *culag* is a seat on the crupper of a horse, and it was quite usual in those days for an old woman to ask a strong young man to give her a lift along the road like this. However, the creature called *bocan-na-crag*—the goblin of the rocks—often takes the shape of an old woman to deceive travelers into giving it a *culag. Bocan-na-crag,* moreover, is another of the strange beings in the service of the *sidhe,* and once it is mounted on a traveler's horse it can never be unseated again. Peigi-Ann was only too well acquainted with these matters, and so she listened

60

in dread as the Skeelie Woman went on,

"MacAllister pities the old woman's weariness, and reaches a hand down to her. He swings her up onto the crupper of his horse, and then—Oh, too late! Too late! He finds it is *bocan-na-crag* he has mounted behind him!"

The spoon began to shake in Peigi-Ann's hand, and a ripple ran over the pool of light in it. "Hold still!" the Skeelie Woman told her sharply. "You are spoiling the picture." Peigi-Ann made a great effort to steady herself. The ripple faded, and the Skeelie Woman peered into the pool again.

"*Bocan-na-crag* is stretching out to seize the reins of MacAllister's horse!" she exclaimed. "He tries to strike its bony hands away. He tries to throw the creature off his horse, but its arms are gripped tight around him. He struggles to free himself, but it is useless—useless! *Bocan-na-crag* has the horse's reins fast in its hands. It urges the beast to a gallop, and the bundle of velvet on the saddle falls to the ground. MacAllister no longer struggles, for now he is completely in the power of *bocan-na-crag*. He is—"

"He is lost to me forever!" Peigi-Ann interrupted wildly, and the stuff in the spoon slopped about with the sobs that shook her.

"You have broken the picture," the Skeelie Woman told her. "I cannot see anything else now."

"It makes no difference," Peigi-Ann sobbed, handing

61

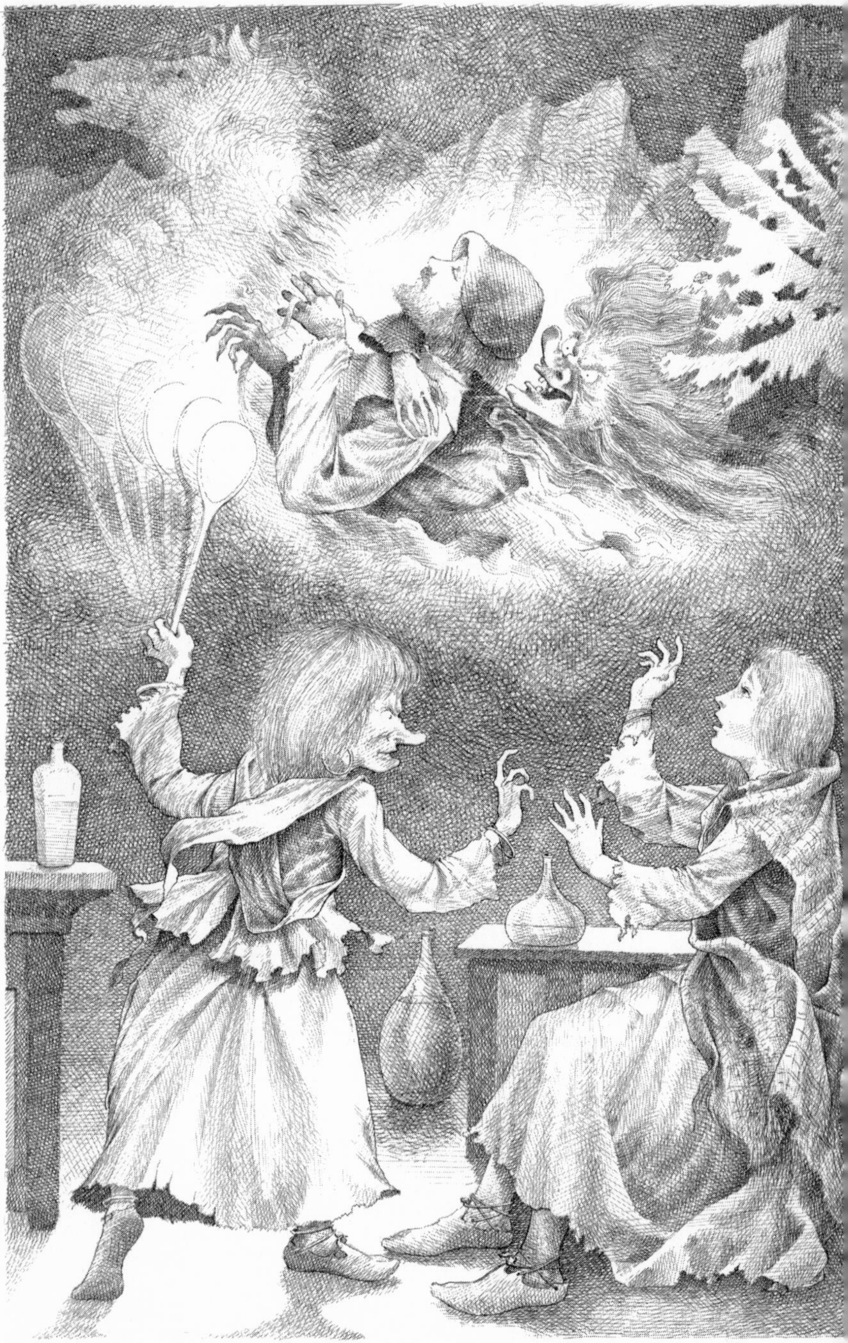

the spoon back to her. "I know what has happened now. My husband has been taken prisoner for the *sidhe* and I shall never see him again."

"I warned him," the Skeelie Woman said, and she sighed. "I warned him, Peigi-Ann, but he was too stubborn to listen to me." She cleaned the spoon and put it away again, and while she was doing this, Peigi-Ann recovered herself a little.

"Supposing," she began to argue, "just supposing I pulled up the hedge around the Goodman's Croft. That would give the *sidhe* what they wanted in the first place, surely, and maybe they would release him then."

The Skeelie Woman shook her head. "Do not deceive yourself, Peigi-Ann," she said sadly. "The *sidhe* never relent once they have made a decision, and they take prisoners for two purposes only. The first is to make slaves of those they capture, and the second—" She stopped, unwilling to go on about this second purpose, but Peigi-Ann urged her,

"Tell me! Tell me the worst, Skeelie Woman."

"If you must hear it then," the Skeelie Woman said with a sigh. "The *sidhe* worship strange gods, Peigi-Ann, and once every seven years these gods demand the sacrifice of a life from them. They will not sacrifice one of their own kind, and so it is a prisoner who must die for them instead."

Peigi-Ann sat still as a stone, looking at her. "Do you

understand?" the Skeelie Woman asked. "Seven years from the time he was captured, Peigi-Ann, MacAllister will die."

"I understand," Peigi-Ann answered. She spoke with difficulty, as if her lips were frozen, then after a long silence she said in the same stiff way, "Tell me your fee now, Skeelie Woman."

The Skeelie Woman looked at her with a tear standing in each of her bright, dark eyes. "Would I take gear or money from a poor widow woman?" she asked. "Would I steal bread from the mouth of a fatherless boy? It is my burden I have the gift to tell you all this, Peigi-Ann. Now go in peace, and may the years ease the pain of your sorrow for you."

Peigi-Ann stood up. "I will not speak of this to anyone," she said, "for fear that Fergus should hear of it."

"I will keep silence also, then," the Skeelie Woman promised.

Peigi-Ann gazed long at her. The Skeelie Woman gazed back like one woman understanding another. Then Peigi-Ann turned away and went homeward, wishing she could die now that she knew her husband was as good as dead, yet knowing she must live for the sake of Fergus. The first thing she did, therefore, was to make the velvet coat that had been promised him, and when it was finished she said,

"Wear it proudly, Fergus, as your father wore his."

64

And because Fergus was too young to grieve for long he was delighted with his coat and wore it with the same proud swagger of MacAllister on his wedding day. Peigi-Ann hid the ache in her heart to smile at him, then she turned to ordering her life as it had to be from then on— as a widow woman.

"We will do the work MacAllister used to do between us," she told Murdo; and Murdo said willingly, "Aye, mistress," for he too had mourned in his simpleminded way for MacAllister.

So for a year and another year, Peigi-Ann worked alongside Murdo every day, planting, sowing, reaping, and tending the beasts; and it was only when she was alone at night that she wept for MacAllister. Her gentle hands grew rough, her back ached and her heart was sore, but at the end of that two years Fergus was big enough to be of some real help to her.

He chopped sticks and fed the hens. With Colm to help him he herded the cattle and guarded the lambs from fox and eagle. He swept out the stable and put fresh hay in the mangers. There were a hundred small jobs a boy could do about the farm, in fact, and Fergus did them well, with Colm like a long gray shadow always trotting watchfully at his side.

Another year passed and another year, and Fergus was nine. Peigi-Ann's days were still long and her nights still sorrowful, but now Fergus was old enough to guide a plow, to cut peats, to stack hay, and to help with the cutting and threshing of the barley crop. His young muscles grew strong. He no longer chattered nonsense with Murdo but discussed the work sensibly, and Peigi-Ann saw that he loved the land and was beginning to look on it with pride as his own.

Then suddenly one day he asked her the questions she had always dreaded he would ask: Why was there a bit of land on the farm that was never planted? And why did it have a hedge of elder and rowan around it?

"It is not planted," she told him shortly, "because it is the custom to leave such a piece of land for the *sidhe*. And it has the hedge around it because your father wished it that way."

Fergus was not satisfied with this answer, but he could see that he would get nothing more out of Peigi-Ann and so he turned his questions on Murdo. Peigi-Ann, of course, had warned Murdo that he must not talk about the Goodman's Croft to Fergus; but being a bit weak in the head, Murdo had forgotten all about her warning and so he told Fergus all about the Urisk and the cross of barley, and also why MacAllister had planted the hedge around the Goodman's Croft.

"That was brave, to defy the *sidhe*," said Fergus, but Murdo shook his head.

"It was just stubborn," he said. "He was an awful stubborn man, MacAllister."

"That is not the way I see it," Fergus told him, and went away with his mind full of the story he had just heard.

"You are to forget all about it—do you hear?" said Peigi-Ann when she discovered Murdo's foolishness. "There are some things that are best forgotten." And to give Fergus a new interest she began to teach him his letters in the evening when the day's work was done.

Fergus was not much of a one for book learning, however, and he much preferred to spend his evenings lying on the hearth beside Colm and staring dreamily into the fire. Moreover, he was always sleepy after his long day in the open air, and what with the warmth of Colm on one side of him and the warmth of the fire on the other the book would drop from his fingers as often as not, and he would fall fast asleep with his head pillowed on Colm's side.

Peigi-Ann had not the heart to wake him when this happened, and so she would sit watching him, seeing how like his father he had grown and thinking that, come what might, she must keep the terrible secret of MacAllister's fate from him. Then she would see how still Colm kept for fear of disturbing Fergus, and her mind would go back to the days when people had said,

"If the March wind can run fast, An Cu Mor can run faster."

It was a pity, she told herself then, that Colm would be

67

too old for a hunting dog before Fergus was old enough to hunt as his father had done; and sadly she would wonder how much longer Fergus could hope to have the creature for his faithful companion.

So Fergus reached the age of ten, and then eleven years, and the taller and stronger he became, the more work he did on the farm. The sorrow of Peigi-Ann's life had put a few threads of silver in the red-gold of her hair by the time he was into his twelfth year, but now she had some leisure too, for Fergus did almost a man's work about the place and he took a man's decisions about it.

There were times, of course, when Peigi-Ann disagreed with his decisions, but she could never win an argument against him for Fergus had his father's stubborn nature as well as his father's looks. Murdo began to notice that she could no longer order Fergus as she had in the past, and one day he said to her,

"You should have married again, mistress. You have had chances enough, goodness knows, and that lad needs a man's firm hand on him."

Now it was true that Peigi-Ann could have married half a dozen times over if she had cared to do so, for she was as beautiful as ever in spite of her silver hairs, and many a young man of the glen had come courting with an eye to her beauty as well as to the farm she would bring with her as her dowry. To all of these, however, Peigi-Ann had said a straightforward "No," and now she told Murdo sharply,

"And you need to mind your own business, Murdo Mathieson. I shall never marry again."

"Never is a long time," Murdo returned, thinking to himself that Peigi-Ann was a great fool to have spoiled so much of her life by staying a widow woman for so long. Nor was he alone in his thought, for the people of the glen could not understand why Peigi-Ann continued to choose the hard lot of a widow when she could have made her life much easier by marrying again.

"She is too proud to take another husband," they said at first, thinking that Peigi-Ann wanted to fly her mourning for MacAllister like a flag in their faces. Then, like Murdo, they decided that she was a fool to work so hard instead of getting a husband to work for her. As the sixth and then the seventh year of MacAllister's disappearance wore on, however, they began to wonder if Peigi-Ann had some secret reason for staying a widow woman.

Some even wondered if she was indeed a widow at all, for they had not forgotten the business of the Goodman's Croft, nor the strange way in which MacAllister had vanished without even a trace of him being found again.

"Maybe MacAllister is not dead after all," they began to whisper among themselves. "Maybe he is a prisoner of the *sidhe*." And soon there was a rumor all around the glen that MacAllister had been "taken," as they call it when someone is stolen by the *sidhe*.

Peigi-Ann heard nothing of this talk, of course, and she was still determined to keep the truth hidden from

Fergus; but with every day that brought her nearer to the end of October that year, she found it harder and harder to live with the knowledge that it was one day nearer to the time of MacAllister's death. She became so pale and silent, indeed, that Fergus thought she must be sickening for some illness, but he had an idea in his mind at the time which stopped him thinking too much about other matters.

It was an idea he had been brooding on for quite a while, and the more he brooded the stronger it grew, until one day just before his twelfth birthday he said to Murdo,

"We are due to start the winter plowing soon, Murdo, and this year I mean to plow the Goodman's Croft too."

"Ach no, Fergus!" Murdo exclaimed in alarm. "You cannot do that."

"Why not?" Fergus demanded. "The land is mine. I can do what I like with it."

"The very words your father once spoke," said Murdo, staring at him. "My, but you are like him, boy!"

"I know that," said Fergus, staring back at Murdo. "My mother has told me so, although she will not speak about the Goodman's Croft. But you must remember my father, Murdo. What else did he say about it?"

Murdo frowned and chewed his lip with the effort of remembering; then at last he said slowly, "I remember the day he brought your mother here as a newlywed lass. He said—he said—*'The land is my life, and nobody is going to take a part of my life from me, or . . .'*"

Murdo stopped, with a look of bewilderment creeping over his poor, daft face, and said helplessly, "I forget the rest, Fergus."

"But I can guess it!" Fergus cried. " '—*or I will be no proper man!*' Eh, Murdo?"

"Aye, aye," Murdo nodded eagerly. "You're right, lad."

"Well, then," Fergus told him, "if I am to take my father's place here, that is all the more reason for me to finish what he started. I *will* plow the Goodman's Croft, Murdo!"

Now Murdo had heard the rumor that was running around the glen, and he was so distressed to hear Fergus speaking like this that, without thinking, he blurted out,

"Then you will be 'taken,' the same as he was."

Fergus stared at him. "Why do you say my father was 'taken'?" he demanded.

"*I* do not say it," poor Murdo told him, all confused at having let the cat out of the bag like this. "People say it— the rest of the people in the glen." And shutting his lips tight for fear another word would escape them, he hurried away and would not come back for all that Fergus called and commanded him.

Fergus went off to the house in the end, turning Murdo's strange words over and over in his mind, and all that evening he was very silent and thoughtful. Peigi-Ann was so wrapped in her own misery, however, that she noticed nothing unusual about him, and they went off to their separate beds that night like two strangers taking leave of one another. Fergus lay for a long time without sleeping, then he heard a noise and sat up in bed to listen.

It was the sound of his mother weeping, he realized, and remembering how he had thought she was sickening for some illness he jumped hastily out of bed to ask her what was wrong. Peigi-Ann, however, would tell him nothing except that she was perfectly well, but Fergus was not so easily put off. He lit the lamp so that he could see her face, then quietly he said,

"I cannot help you until I know what troubles you. And it is my place to put trouble right, for I am the man of the house."

"You are not a man until you have learned that a woman will sometimes weep for no good reason," Peigi-Ann retorted. "Now go back to bed and get some sleep."

"I have all my life to sleep," Fergus told her, and she cried,

"Och! You are as stubborn as your father!"

"You said that," said Fergus, "as if he were still alive."

The tears started from Peigi-Ann again at this, and Fergus went on, "Indeed, you are not the only one to talk like that, for there is a whisper going around the glen, and it says he is not dead but 'taken.' "

"You have no business listening to such idle gossip!" Peigi-Ann cried, but Fergus knew instantly from the look on her face that he had hit on the truth. Question her as he would after this, however, Peigi-Ann still would not admit to knowing anything more, for she was still trying to spare Fergus the grief of learning that his father was soon to die. Fergus, for his part, was not prepared to let the matter rest there, and so he told her,

"If my father has indeed been 'taken,' there is only one thing to do about it. He must be won back again."

"You stupid boy!" Peigi-Ann snapped. "Do you think I would have suffered like this for seven years if I could have thought of any way he might be rescued from the *sidhe?*"

"I am not blaming you," said Fergus reasonably. "I am just telling you what must be done now."

"Do you know what you are saying?" Peigi-Ann cried. "There is not a man in the glen would dare to try such a thing!"

"I know that," Fergus answered, "but *I* am not afraid to try."

"No!" cried Peigi-Ann. "No, Fergus! I do not want to lose you too. And besides, you have not the least idea of how to set about such a business."

"I know that too," Fergus told her, "but I will soon find someone who will make me wiser."

And dressing himself quickly, in spite of all her protests he went up the glen to see the Skeelie Woman.

6

THE SKEELIE WOMAN

"I have been expecting you," the Skeelie Woman said when Fergus came to her door, and he wondered how this could be.

"Then you must know why I have come," he told her.

The Skeelie Woman smiled. "You have a sharp mind," she remarked, "but it will take more than that to do what you are planning to do!"

She led the way into her kitchen and sat herself down beside the light of the one candle in it. "Now," she said, "speak up, boy."

Fergus looked into her glittering dark eyes and felt a touch of fear at their strangeness, but still stuck boldly to his purpose. "Is it true," he asked, "that my father is not dead, but has been taken by the *sidhe*?"

The Skeelie Woman nodded. "Yes, that is true. Mac-

74

Allister was taken nearly seven years ago, and he has been a slave to the *sidhe* since then."

"Will they ever free him?" Fergus asked.

"No," the Skeelie Woman answered. "His slavery will last the full seven years, and then the *sidhe* will sacrifice him to the dark gods of their magic."

Fergus gasped at this, and breathlessly he cried, "But how do you know? How can you be so certain that will happen?"

"It is the custom of the *sidhe*," the Skeelie Woman told him, but Fergus said stubbornly,

"Then they must do without their custom for once, for I mean to rescue him."

The Skeelie Woman looked him up and down. "And if I tell you how to do that," she said, "what will you pay me?"

"Anything you ask!" Fergus exclaimed.

"Anything?" she repeated.

"Yes, anything," he insisted. "Even if I have to work all my life to earn it."

"You will not have to do that," the Skeelie Woman told him. "Indeed, you may not even live to pay my fee. Will you risk that?"

"I told you," Fergus said. "I will pay you anything you ask, and risk any danger to earn your fee."

"I see you are as stubborn as your father," the Skeelie Woman remarked, and Fergus answered,

"So my mother has already told me."

"Ah well, if you have the rest of his nature too, you'll make a man some day," the Skeelie Woman said drily. "But in the meantime, let us see where MacAllister is and what he is doing."

With that, she rose to fetch her silver spoon, and gave it to Fergus to hold to the candlelight, as she had given it to Peigi-Ann. Then she filled it with the dark liquid, and Fergus saw the point of candlelight gleaming on this darkness beginning to spread and turn paler, until it seemed he was holding a pool of clear light in his hand. He peered into this, as the Skeelie Woman was peering, but could see nothing there. Disappointed, he said,

"There is nothing to be seen, Skeelie Woman."

She hushed him to silence, staring and occasionally muttering to herself; then suddenly she reached out to take the spoon from him, and said,

"Enough! I have seen all that my gift will allow me to see."

Puzzled, Fergus watched her empty the spoon and put it away again, and when she turned once more toward him he saw that she was holding something clenched tightly in her fist.

"What did you see in the spoon, Skeelie Woman?" he asked, and watched the clenched fist by her side.

The Skeelie Woman gave him question for question. "Tell me, Fergus," she said, "have you ever heard of the treasure of the *sidhe*?"

76

"No," Fergus told her wonderingly. "I never have."

"Then look here," said the Skeelie Woman, and opening her hand she held it out to him, palm upward. Fergus stared, for on her palm lay a little cluster of jewels that glittered in every shade of yellow, from the palest honey-gold to a deep, dark, golden-bronze; and watching Fergus stare at these, the Skeelie Woman said,

"These are cairngorms, Fergus; the yellow gemstones that are quarried from the rock of the Cairngorm Mountains. *These* are the treasure of the *sidhe*. They have caves and caves full of them, all quarried by the labor of the people they have taken. And that is how your father has spent the years of his captivity. That is what he is doing now. He is chained to the rocks at the summit of Ben MacDui, while he works night and day to quarry more treasure for the *sidhe*."

Fergus looked curiously from the glittering gold jewels of the mountain to the glittering dark eyes of the Skeelie Woman. "And how do *you* come to have this little part of their treasure?" he asked.

"My mother was a woman of the *sidhe*," she said quietly. "I had the jewels from her, along with the gift that lets me see times past and times still to come when you can see nothing at all in my silver spoon."

Slowly she closed her hand over the jewels, sighing and shaking her head so that her silver earrings twinkled. "But that is all I had, for my father was a mortal man. And so, although I can look in my spoon and see the beautiful world of the *sidhe*, I can never enter that world."

There was a look of bitter longing on her face as she spoke these words and Fergus thought it must be a terrible thing to be someone who did not belong either to the human world or the other world of the *sidhe*. All the same, he could understand now how the Skeelie Woman had known he would come to see her, and so he was eager to hear what else she could tell him.

"And how can I rescue my father from the *sidhe*?" he asked. "You have still to tell me that for your fee."

"That will be a lot more dangerous to try than you could ever imagine," the Skeelie Woman warned, "for he is guarded by the same creature as guards the treasure of the *sidhe*. *An Ferla Mor*—the Great Gray Man, it is called, because it has the form of a man although it is made entirely of gray stone and is three times the size of an ordinary man. Moreover, it is armed with a great sword that has a single ray of light for its blade, and the only way it can be destroyed is by a stroke from that same sword of light."

Fergus stared in dismay at all this, but still the Skeelie Woman went on, "You must know also, Fergus, that An Ferla Mor never sleeps, but roams constantly over the slopes of Ben MacDui, and the mere sight of him will send the bravest man running away in terror. Yet fast as he may run, he still cannot escape the power of An Ferla Mor, for it will be a blind and nameless panic that grips him, and this panic will send him running straight toward his death over the lip of the great cliff called The Lurcher's Crag."

Fergus felt his heart sink even further while he listened to this last warning, but he was a boy of great common sense and so he argued,

"But surely this Ferla Mor must have some weak spot, Skeelie Woman. Otherwise, you would not have bothered to tell me all this. You would just have said it is not possible to rescue my father."

"Oh, aye, he has a weak spot," the Skeelie Woman agreed. "An Ferla Mor is blind! But his ears are so sharp that he can hear the grass grow, and so there is only one safety for you if he should hear your footsteps and come after you. You must stay as still and silent as the mountain itself until he has passed by you."

"I will do that all right, I promise you!" Fergus exclaimed. "Now tell me how I can make sure he does *not* hear me walking on Ben MacDui."

"There is no way you can make entirely sure of that," the Skeelie Woman said. "But you can be fairly sure of avoiding him on the way up to the summit of Ben MacDui if you also avoid all the well-known ways to that point, for these are the ways he guards most closely. What *you* must do, therefore, is to climb up to the summit by way of the stream called the March Burn, which is a way that few people would ever consider taking."

"You will have to describe it to me, then," Fergus told her, "for I have only seen Ben MacDui at a distance before this, and I have no idea where the March Burn is."

"You will easily find it," the Skeelie Woman told him, "if you follow these directions. Take the path that leads from this glen into the Lairig Ghru, and climb to the summit of the pass. That means you will be traveling south, with a touch of east in your direction, and so The Lurcher's Crag and the other high cliffs of Ben MacDui's west face will be on your left hand.

"Go on for half a mile down the defile beyond the summit of the pass, and then you will see the March Burn tumbling down the cliffs that will still be on your left hand. Climb to the top of these cliffs by way of the burn—which should take you about two hours to do— then turn sharp right so that you are facing the summit of Ben MacDui. It will take you another two hours at least of walking and climbing to reach the summit, and there you will find MacAllister, chained with golden chains to the rock of the quarry where he digs for the jewels."

"And how can I break these chains?" Fergus interrupted in dismay. "How is it my father has never been able to break them? I have heard he was reckoned a strong man."

The Skeelie Woman gave a scornful little smile. "There is *no* human strength can break these chains!" she exclaimed. "Indeed, there is no creature on earth that can defeat the power which the magic of the *sidhe* has given them."

"Then what can I do about them?" Fergus asked helplessly. "What *can* I do?"

"Be quiet, will you, and listen!" the Skeelie Woman told him sharply. "The day after tomorrow is Hallowe'en, and there are only two nights in the year when a person who has been taken by the *sidhe* can be won back from them—Midsummer's Eve, and Hallowe'en. Moreover, there is only one hour in each of these nights when such an attempt at rescue can succeed, and that is the first hour of true darkness. Do you understand?"

"I do," said Fergus, and felt his heart sink again as he realized he would not be able to keep a lookout for An Ferla Mor in the darkness of the journey back from the summit of Ben MacDui.

"Then understand this also," the Skeelie Woman said grimly. "The whole kingdom of the *sidhe* will be abroad in the first hour of darkness on Hallowe'en, and they will use all the force of their magic against you. But if you seize tight hold of MacAllister's hand, and keep your grip on it no matter what happens, he will be freed from the power of the *sidhe* and the golden chains will drop from him of their own accord."

"That sounds too easy," Fergus said suspiciously. "What will they do to make me let go of his hand?"

The Skeelie Woman shook her head. "You will not find it easy," she warned. "You will find it very hard to bear the terrible things the magic of the *sidhe* will do to you then. Can you stand pain, Fergus?"

81

"I can try," Fergus said in a small voice. Then he felt ashamed at sounding so faint-hearted, and added loudly, "I *will* try!"

The Skeelie Woman's eyes gleamed, and he remembered the fee he had promised her—"*Anything!*"

"Now ask what you want of me," he told her. "I am ready to pay your fee."

"I want more of these!" the Skeelie Woman exclaimed, holding up her fist with the little store of cairngorms clenched in it. "Bring me more of them, Fergus—bring me a great double handful of them! If I cannot be part of the world of the *sidhe*, I want some of the treasure that belongs to it. I want rings of jewels, Fergus; necklaces of jewels, bracelets, brooches of jewels. I want to walk in such a blaze of golden jewels that the people of the glen will not look at my brown, wrinkled skin anymore, but at the splendor of my jewels. I am ugly, Fergus—I know I am ugly; but my mother's people are beautiful and I want at least to be able to walk in beauty before I die."

Fergus shivered and backed away from the Skeelie Woman, for in her eagerness, she was clutching at him as she spoke. Firmly he put her hand aside, and coldly he said,

"So that is why you have been so ready to help me! You do not care whether or not my father is rescued. You do not care if I am killed by An Ferla Mor. All you want is your fee in jewels!"

"That is not so," the Skeelie Woman answered, and the glitter faded from her dark eyes. "Seven years ago I promised your mother I would keep silence over what I knew, so that you would never learn your father's fate. But when I knew you wanted to rescue him, I thought it only right that you should at least have the chance to try. For after all, Fergus, my own father was a mortal man and so I have some human feelings."

Fergus looked at the sadness in her shriveled brown face and felt sorry for his harsh words. "I misjudged you, Skeelie Woman," he said. "I am sorry for the way I spoke, and if I escape alive from Ben MacDui I will bring you all the fee you could desire."

"Then listen to this last word of advice," the Skeelie Woman told him. "Your mother will ask you a question before you go and you must think hard before you answer it; for if you answer it wrongly, you will have no hope of succeeding in what you intend to do. But if you give the correct answer it will be the best protection you could possibly have against the dangers you will meet."

"Then tell me what the question is," Fergus urged. "And if you want to be sure of your jewels, tell me what I should answer to it."

"No!" the Skeelie Woman said, and shook her head till her silver earrings danced like stars. "No, no, no, Fergus! There are rules to magic as there are rules to everything. If you break the rule the magic loses its power, and the rule of the question is that you, yourself, must find the right answer to it."

She picked up her candle to show Fergus to the door. "Now remember," she warned as she opened it for him. "It is a long journey you have ahead of you, and so you must leave yourself plenty of time to reach the summit of Ben MacDui before darkness falls."

"I will set out in good time," Fergus assured her, and took his leave of her wondering what his mother would say to all the news he had to tell.

7

ON THE MOUNTAIN (I)

Peigi-Ann had been having a good think to herself while Fergus was visiting the Skeelie Woman, and she soon realized there was nothing she could do to stop him going after his father. She decided to make the best of a bad job, therefore, and when Fergus arrived home he found her up and dressed and looking her usual self again. She listened carefully to all he had to tell, and although her heart turned over at the mere mention of An Ferla Mor, she did not argue any further against the idea of trying to rescue MacAllister.

"If you must go, you must go," was all she said then. "But tell Murdo to see your pony is well shod, for it is a rough journey you will have along the Lairig Ghru."

Fergus went out to see to his pony, and Peigi-Ann set about her work as usual. She was used to sorrow by this time after all, she told herself, and if Fergus was to keep his courage up she must not let him see her grieving. Little else was said between them that day, therefore, but many a time Peigi-Ann found herself glancing toward the Goodman's Croft and thinking of the terrible ruin it had made of all their lives.

"I will bake a bannock for you to eat on your journey," she told Fergus that afternoon, and he said,

"Make it a big one, then, for I shall be a whole day and a night on the road."

Peigi-Ann said nothing to this. She got out the oatmeal and salt, and the griddle for baking the bannock, but all the time she was making the dough for it she was thinking of the question the Skeelie Woman had said she would ask Fergus before he left home. Peigi-Ann knew very well that the question had to do with the bannock she was baking. She knew also that a Highland woman must always ask this same question of any son or daughter who might be leaving home for the last time; but she was afraid that Fergus would answer it wrongly and so she took no pleasure in the baking of that bannock.

She set the bannock to cool while she made the supper, then for a long time after they had eaten, she and Fergus talked together. It was of MacAllister himself that they talked—the first time that Peigi-Ann had really opened her heart to Fergus about him—and he listened entranced while she spoke of that wild night in the Lairig Ghru when he had twice outwitted the *sidhe*; and of the morning afterward when he had come striding toward her with a glorious madness of love and triumph on his face.

"There was a man!" she said with a sigh. "There was a *man*, Fergus!"

"I wish I had known all this before," Fergus answered, his eyes shining. "I would have gone all the sooner to rescue him!"

It was his turn to talk then, and he sounded so sure he could rescue MacAllister that Peigi-Ann went to bed feeling much happier as a result. Fergus himself, however, lay awake for a long time that night, for much as he wanted to rescue his father he was still very afraid of An Ferla Mor, and it was only to spare his mother's feelings that he had made himself sound much braver than he had really felt.

The next morning was the morning of Hallowe'en, and time for Fergus to start his journey. Murdo brought his pony to the door while Peigi-Ann went over the directions the Skeelie Woman had given him. Then she picked up the flat cake of the bannock and broke it into two pieces. One of the pieces was bigger than the other, and she held them both out to Fergus.

"Whether will you have the big half with my curse," she asked, "or the little half with my blessing?"

Fergus was about to say, "The big half," thinking of the long day that lay ahead of him. Then he remembered the

87

Skeelie Woman had said his mother would ask him a question before he left, and had warned him also of the importance of answering it correctly. He hesitated, thinking he could not feel happy setting out on such a journey with his mother's curse instead of her blessing—but he was sure to be hungry before the day was out if he chose the little half! He hesitated still more, and then made up his mind quickly.

"I will have the little half with your blessing," he said.

Peigi-Ann smiled with relief and handed him the small half of the bannock. "Take it then," she said, "and when danger strikes, remember that my blessing lies between you and all harm."

Fergus put the bannock in his pouch and went to the door. Colm rose to his feet—slowly, because he was such a very old dog by this time—and followed him outside. Peigi-Ann shook her head at this, and caught hold of Colm as Fergus mounted his pony. Colm tried to break away to take his usual place alongside the pony, but Peigi-Ann said firmly,

"No, Colm. You are too old for such a journey."

Fergus gathered the reins in his hands. Colm whined pitifully at the thought of being left behind, and Fergus hesitated.

"He would be company for me at least," he said, feeling sorry for the old dog.

"He would only hold you back," Peigi-Ann objected,

and while they were still arguing like this over whether or not Colm should go with him, the Skeelie Woman appeared.

"I brought you this," she said to Fergus, holding up a little arrow-shaped piece of flintstone set in silver. "It is a charm against the bite of poisonous snakes. There are a lot of adders in the Lairig Ghru, and on Ben MacDui."

Fergus thanked her and put the charm in his pocket. Colm was still straining to reach him and the Skeelie Woman noticed this. "Let him go with Fergus," she told Peigi-Ann.

"He will be no use to the boy," Peigi-Ann protested, but the Skeelie Woman only repeated,

"Let him go, Peigi-Ann."

Peigi-Ann tried once more. "He is old—an old, done creature, that is all," she said.

The Skeelie Woman shook her head. "You are wrong, Peigi-Ann," she answered. "The day of An Cu Mor is not yet over. Let him go with Fergus."

She fixed Peigi-Ann with the stare of her strange, dark eyes, and slowly Peigi-Ann let go her grip on Colm. He bounded stiffly forward on his old legs, and Fergus urged his pony to a walk. Colm took his place alongside it, the pony broke into a trot along the path leading out of the glen, and Fergus turned in the saddle to wave good-bye.

"You will see me home again this time tomorrow morning," he cried cheerfully. "With my father!"

"Please God," Peigi-Ann added quietly.

The Skeelie Woman tried to say "Amen," but being only half human the word stuck in her throat, and she went slowly back to her own house while Peigi-Ann watched Fergus out of sight.

It was a fine morning—as mornings in late October often are in the Highlands—with just a touch of frost in the air and a sky of blue and gold with hardly a cloud in it. Fergus rode along cheerfully, feeling the sun warm on his face as he set it south toward the Lairig Ghru and wondering at the color of the Cairngorm Mountains ahead of him.

They looked blue from this distance, he thought, a deep, dark—almost a navy blue, and he decided they had been very well named, for *cairn* is a Gaelic word meaning rock, and *gorm* is the Gaelic for blue.

The sun was high in the sky before he came in sight of the Lairig Ghru itself, opening out in a great V-shape between Ben MacDui on his left hand and the mountain called Braeriach on his right. Fergus put his pony boldly to the beginning of the track leading into the V, and made good progress along it.

The track grew rougher after a while, and began to climb steeper and ever steeper. The pony's pace dropped to a slow plod, and sometimes it had to stop altogether while Fergus peered for a sign of the track among the litter of stones that hid it. The frowning cliffs of Ben

MacDui to the left and the towering height of Braeriach to the right shut out the sun. The air grew colder. The day grew older. And still Fergus had not reached the head of the pass.

The time was wearing on fast—too fast, he thought as he passed by the grim rock face of The Lurcher's Crag jutting from Ben MacDui. And the way was becoming too rough for even a surefooted beast like his pony, for now the track had disappeared completely under the stones that lay thick over the last mile to the head of the pass. As for Colm, his mother had been right when she said not to take him, for he was no longer An Cu Mor, the great hunter. He was only an old, done creature trailing listlessly along, and it was nothing short of a nuisance to have him there!

Everything must come to an end sometime, however, and soon after these thoughts went through his head, the end of the climb came for Fergus. He found himself at the highest point of the pass, and knew he had only another mile or so to ride before he saw the March Burn. He paused to look around before he began the ride down the rocky defile ahead.

There was only one sound to break the stillness of the air at that high point—the faint sound of running water that came from little mountain torrents dropping sharply here and there over the red granite cliffs of Ben MacDui. Yet somehow this one sound seemed to make the surrounding silence all the deeper, and Fergus was suddenly glad that he *had* taken Colm for company.

"Not long now, boy," he said encouragingly. Colm turned wise old eyes on him as if he understood this remark, and they began the descent to the March Burn.

Fergus saw it on his left hand less than half an hour later—a torrent of water gushing and tumbling over the cliffs—and stopped at the foot of it. He tied his pony to a rock there, then took out his bannock and ate it, giving Colm a little piece as his share. Then he took a drink of water from the burn, and looked at the climb ahead of him.

It was steep, he saw, but not too steep for someone like himself, born and bred to mountain country. He set his foot to the rock, and Colm also began to scramble upward.

"Go back!" Fergus said sharply, thinking it would never do to have the old dog hampering him now, and Colm went sadly back.

Fergus began to climb. A few minutes later he looked down and saw that Colm was following him again. It was not like Colm to be disobedient, and uneasily he remembered the Skeelie Woman saying,

The day of An Cu Mor is not yet over.

He had better let matters take their course, Fergus decided, and perhaps he would find a use for Colm yet. He set himself to the climb again, and labored on, hearing Colm's nails scratch on the rocks as he scrambled up in the rear. There were good handholds among the rocks, he found, just as he had thought there would be; but there were also the snakes the Skeelie Woman had warned against!

Every now and then he glimpsed the gleam of scales in some crevice of the rock, and snatched away his hand before the adder's diamond-patterned head could come poking out of the gloom. Every now and then he saw the yellow-and-black zig-zag of an adder's body slithering smooth and silent over the rocks. Every now and then he glimpsed eyes, small, cold, and yellow, watching him as he climbed. But the Skeelie Woman's charm must have protected him, for although some of the adders came close, none of them struck at him.

Between keeping a lookout for these creatures, however, and the difficulties of the climb itself, Fergus had little time to spare for thoughts of An Ferla Mor. It was only when he reached the end of his climb that he gave serious thought to that danger, for it was then that he turned his face toward the summit of Ben MacDui and realized what still lay before him.

It was a gray and cloudy day now, but for miles and miles ahead, he could see, there was a great waste of bare, rocky ground, all ridged with great boulders sticking out of it and pitted with great craters plunging down. Not a tree, not a bush grew there to soften its harshness. It was a wild and barren place, a place as lonely as a desert.

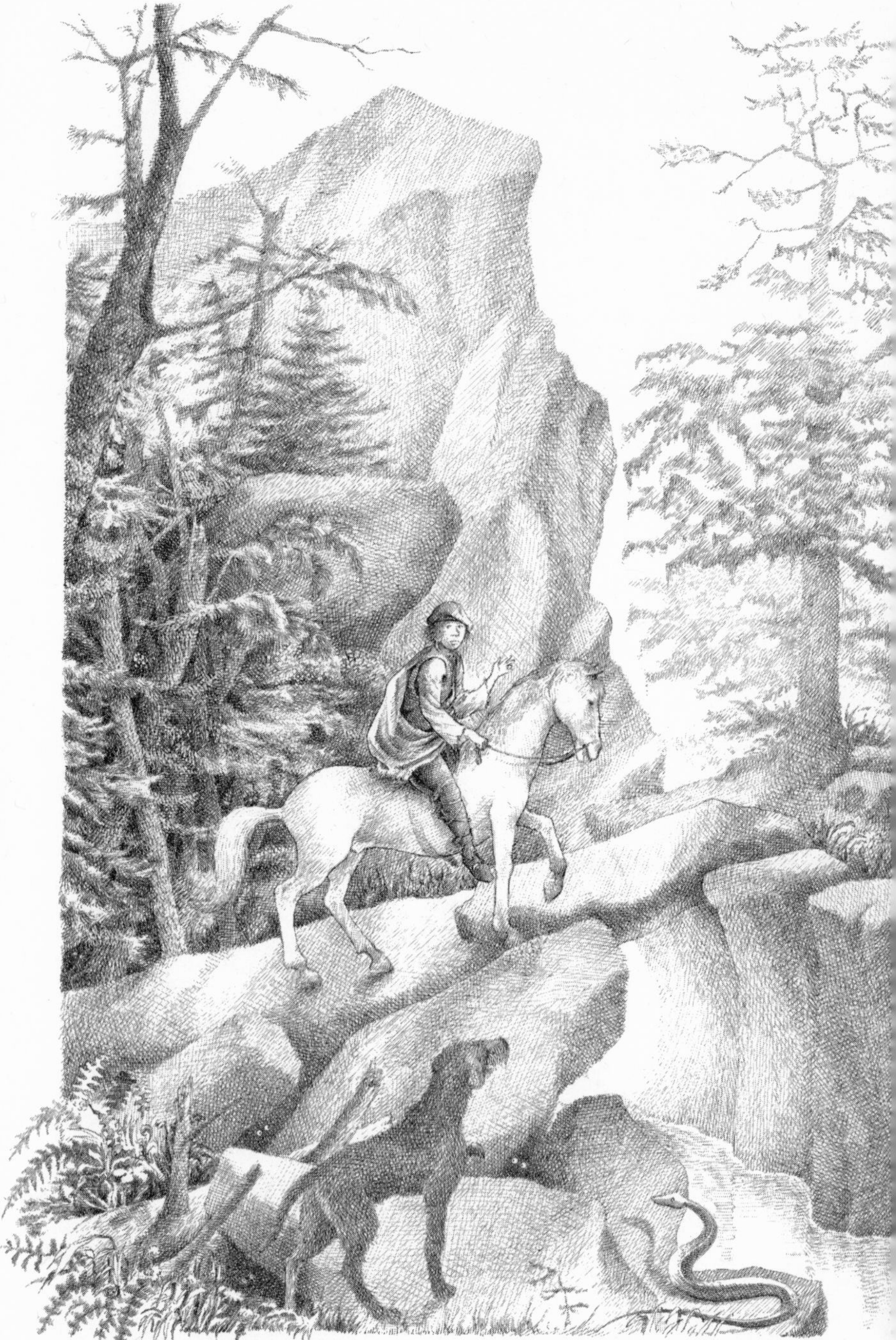

Fergus stared in dismay, imagining he saw An Ferla Mor in every one of the huge boulders jutting out of the ground; imagining how clearly An Ferla Mor would hear his own footsteps ringing on the rock of this desolate wasteland. A moaning sound struck his ear and he jumped in terror, then realized it was only the wind among the rocks he could hear.

Colm growled softly, sensing the fear that was in him, and Fergus put out a hand to quiet him. The touch of the rough gray coat made him feel safe, as it had done when he was a little boy. Besides which, he reminded himself, he had his mother's blessing between himself and all harm.

"Come on, then," he told Colm, and putting his foot forward on the word, he started off for the summit of Ben MacDui.

Two hours, the Skeelie Woman had said this part of the journey would take him, but Fergus walked and climbed for an hour and then another hour and still he had not reached the summit. And the day was beginning to fade! Fergus glanced anxiously at the sky. He was wasting too much time in keeping a lookout for An Ferla Mor, he decided, and fixing his eyes on the great heap of rocks marking the summit of the mountain he walked on as fast as he could go.

He came up to this point at last, panting, the muscles of his legs trembling with effort, and saw that he still had enough daylight left to begin the search for his father. But where, in all this wild jumble of rock around the summit, was he to start looking? Fergus stood biting his lip as he asked himself this question, then almost laughed aloud as he realized suddenly how simple an answer it had. If anyone could find MacAllister, it would be his own hunting dog! He looked down at Colm.

"Hi, seek, boy!" he said softly. "On you go! Seek! Seek! Hi, seek!"

Colm started off, nose to the ground, and Fergus watched him anxiously. Round and round Colm cast, in a small circle at first, then a larger one, and a larger one still; every circle cutting through the one he had made before, yet always covering a much bigger area of fresh ground. Fergus went slowly after him as he drew farther and farther from the summit, then found he was losing sight of Colm altogether as the creature disappeared into the deep pits among the rocks on the west side of the summit. But Colm was onto some scent! He could hear him yelping now!

Fergus followed in the direction of the sound, scrambling, slipping, climbing, running, in a fury of haste. Colm yelped again, then he howled, a long sobbing howl. Fergus paused to listen. The sound of the howl died away and a voice called out in the silence that followed it—a man's voice!

Fergus ran again, calling, shouting now in his excitement, and found himself brought up short at last on the lip of a great quarry among the rocks. He stared down into the quarry, and saw Colm there leaping and yelping around the figure of a man—a tall man, chained with long golden chains to the rocks around him, with his hair and his beard grown long and his clothes in rags. The man was looking up toward him.

"I'm coming! I'm coming!" Fergus shouted, quite forgetting in his excitement that his father could not see who he was at that distance—and quite forgetting also that An Ferla Mor might hear all the noise he and Colm were making. He slithered and jumped down the side of the quarry, and ran, stumbling, toward his father; then stopped short of him, feeling suddenly shy.

He had been only a very small boy, after all, when his father was taken, and so he could not remember what he looked like. Moreover, he could hardly see this man's face for the long dark hair tumbling about it, and the beard that hid half of it. But the chains were there, fastening him by the wrists and ankles to the rock. And Colm certainly seemed to know him! Fergus plucked up his courage again.

"Are you—are you MacAllister?" he asked cautiously.

The big man was staring at him so hard that he blushed, and looked down at the hammer and chisel lying on the ground. Then he stared at the great pile of cairngorms beside the tools, some in clusters the size of his fist and others

97

small and separate, but all shining gold and bright against the granite rock of the quarry. The big man had still not answered him. Fergus looked up again, and their eyes met.

"Yes," the big man said. "I am MacAllister. But I do not need to ask who *you* are. I can see the likeness to myself in you—Fergus!"

He began to move forward but the chains around his ankles pulled him up short. He held out his hands and said quietly, "Come here, Fergus."

Fergus came shyly toward him and his father enfolded him in a great hug, while Colm whined and jumped around the two of them.

"Is your mother alive? Is she well?" MacAllister asked then.

"Aye, she's alive and well," Fergus answered, still breathless from the mighty hug his father had given him. "But she never told me you had a big beard!"

MacAllister laughed. "So would you have a big beard if you were a man that had not touched a razor in seven years," he retorted. His face grew grave again and he went on, "But listen, Fergus, I do not know how you came to be on this mountain, but you must go away again quickly, or An Ferla Mor will get you."

"No!" Fergus cried. "No! I came to rescue you!"

"What!" MacAllister stared in amazement.

"I came to rescue you before the *sidhe* can kill you,"

Fergus repeated, and as quickly as he could then, he told his father everything that had happened since he went to see the Skeelie Woman.

MacAllister shook his head in wonder as he listened, but when Fergus had finished he said sadly, "Aye, you are a brave lad, right enough; as brave as I could ever wish for a son. But even so, you would still feel a terrible fear when the *sidhe* came at you with all their power, and so you could never stand against the force of their magic."

"I will not be afraid," Fergus assured him. "I have my mother's blessing between me and all harm, and that will protect me."

MacAllister gave a little groan, then softly to himself he said, "Peigi-Ann! Oh, my Peigi-Ann! What it must have cost you to let the boy go out alone like this!"

He looked at Fergus again. "Now listen, boy," he said, "it is true your mother's blessing will be a powerful protection to you when you seize my hand to win me back from the *sidhe*; but this will only last *as long as you manage to keep your grip on me*. If they can force you to let my hand go, it will mean that their magic has conquered the power of human love in her blessing. You will become their prisoner then also, and so our last case will be worse than our first."

"I will not let go," Fergus declared. "I promise you that."

"But you do not know the things they will do to make

you let go!" MacAllister cried. "Terrible things, Fergus. You will feel pain such as you never dreamed of, and feel terror too strong for any human soul to endure. I cannot let you face that, and so away you go now, and tell your mother I loved her to the end."

"It is not the end yet," Fergus answered stubbornly, "and I *will* hold on to you no matter how the *sidhe* try to make me loose my grip."

MacAllister gave an anxious glance up to the sky, darkening now with the coming night. "If you will not think of your own safety," he urged, "think of your mother and try to save yourself for her sake."

"My mother would not want me to turn back now," said Fergus, "or she would not have let me go in the first place."

MacAllister changed his tune at this, for now he saw that it was useless trying to persuade Fergus. "A son must do as his father bids," he said sternly, "and I order you to go now."

"You cannot order me against my conscience," Fergus objected. "Besides, would *you* give in to the *sidhe* in spite of all they have done to you?"

"Never!" MacAllister exclaimed, and raised both arms to shake his fists at the sky. "Not supposing they keep me in slavery for seven times seven years!"

Fergus gazed up at the great chained figure towering above him in the gray dark. "They will not do that," he reminded it. "It is your life itself they want now."

"Let them take that too if they must," MacAllister retorted. "They will still be defeated for they have still not managed to get my land."

"And they never will," Fergus told him, "for *I* will never give it to them."

"Well!" said MacAllister. "Well! I see that we are two of a kind, boy. And if that is the way of things, then you do have the right to stay now if you choose."

"Give me your hand then—quickly!" Fergus cried. "The first hour of darkness has begun!"

8

ON THE MOUNTAIN (II)

MacAllister and his son stood hand in hand, shivering in the cold wind that moaned over the dark mountainside. MacAllister's hand was warm and Fergus felt safe clutching it, but he did not feel so safe when his father said,

"Whatever happens, Fergus, remember that it *is* my hand you are holding."

"I will remember," Fergus answered through chattering teeth, for now the cold wind was blowing colder still. Its moaning rose to a sudden shriek, and MacAllister cried,

"They are coming, Fergus! The *sidhe* are coming! Hold on tight!"

Fergus held on. The wind's voice grew shriller still. His father's hand became cold as a block of ice suddenly—so cold that he could hardly bear the feel of it. The wind tore at his clothes. It plucked at his hair like sharp, clawing hands. There *were* hands tearing at him, he realized in sudden terror—dozens of invisible hands with fingers as sharp as birds' claws! The single voice of the wind had become hundreds of high-pitched voices shrieking around him; the single force of it against his body had suddenly become hundreds of blows from invisible creatures attacking him from all directions.

"They are here!" He tried to shout the words but all the breath was being knocked out of him, and all he could do was gasp. He fell to his knees under the force of the blows landing on him, and the creatures attacking him beat and whirled and flapped around his head like giant, invisible bats. He choked and gasped for air, and tried to shout to his father for help, but somehow his father seemed to have vanished and the icy hand he held had indeed become nothing but a block of ice.

The ice slipped and slithered in his grasp, and he was about to throw it from him when he recalled his father's warning, *"Remember it is my hand you are holding."* He clutched the ice harder still, gasping at the burning cold of it against his skin, and wedged it against his chest to keep it from slipping.

The shape of the ice changed under his fingers, stretching and twisting with a life of its own. Despairingly Fergus tried to hold it steady, then discovered to his horror that it was no longer a block of ice he was clutching to his

103

chest, but a snake! And the snake was growing under his hands, growing—growing into a four-foot-long adder darting a poisonous head at him.

With a shout of alarm Fergus gripped it just below the head with one hand, and clamped his other hand around its wriggling body. The wild voices of the *sidhe* were still screaming in his ears. Their invisible shapes still crowded around, pushing, jostling, sending him blundering about in every direction. The snake hissed and threshed in his grip, and gasping with fear now, he felt his footing go from him and crashed to the ground.

Rolling about among the rocks of the quarry, he wrestled madly to keep his grip on the snake; but still, in spite of his panic, he managed to hold on to one thought. It was not a real snake he was holding. It was his father magicked into the appearance of a snake. And whether it was this thought that helped him, or whether it was the charm the Skeelie Woman had given him, the twisting and wriggling of the snake gradually stopped and he lay alone in the darkness with something that felt like a dry stick in his hands.

The voices of the *sidhe* were still also. They were no longer tormenting him with their clawing and beating. There was a dead silence on the mountaintop. Sighing, Fergus rose to his feet—and the stick he was holding burst fiercely into flame along its entire length.

Fergus yelled; in panic at first, and then in pain as the

hot flames ran along his hands and wrists. He held the blazing stick as far away from himself as he could, desperately telling himself that the fire was not real fire and that the pain of the burns he could feel did not come from real burns. It was still his father's hand he was holding, he reminded himself, but the stick burned fiercer than ever and the flames from it licked at his clothes.

"*I will burn to death!*" he thought wildly, and the terror that gripped him became almost more than he could bear.

The flames flared up all around him, and over his head. He was like a human torch blazing in the night; but even in the midst of this terror he could see that his clothes had not caught fire after all. He was not burning to death! And, he realized then, this could not happen so long as his hold on the blazing stick kept his mother's blessing between himself and all harm!

His terror ebbed. He set his teeth to endure the fierce pain of the burns that were not real burns, and held on until he was blind and sobbing with the agony of it. Smoke began to waver around the flames. It was a grayish-black smoke that grew thicker and thicker until it smothered the flames, and the blaze of the stick itself died away into smoke also. A shape formed out of the smoke curling between his fingers.

The shape became solid and twisted fiercely in his hands. The gray smoke had become gray fur, and he could feel the movement of powerful muscles underneath it. Claws raked the skin of his wrists. Sharp teeth sank into the flesh of his hands. It was the wriggling, spitting, fighting body of a wildcat he was clutching now!

Fergus gripped it by the scruff of the neck with one hand and dug the fingers of his other hand into the fur of its back; but for its size, there is no fiercer creature living than the wildcat of the Scottish mountains, and holding this one was like holding a tiger by the tail. Fergus hung on with all his strength, digging his fingers ever deeper into the creature's fur and dodging his head from side to side to avoid the claws that came slashing toward his eyes.

The wildcat snarled and yelled its rage. Its fur stood on end. Its eyes blazed at him. Then suddenly Fergus felt the spikes of soft fur becoming hard and needle-pointed. The creature itself shrank under his hands, and he found himself holding the spiny body of a hedgehog with all its prickles erect and pressing sharply into the soft flesh of his palms.

Fergus groaned aloud at the first taste of this new form of torment, but still he did not yield an inch of his grip. Indeed, he held harder than ever; for if he could endure the fire, he told himself, he could endure anything. He pressed firmly against the sharp prickles, then cried out in horror as he discovered that the hedgehog had suddenly become a huge, slimy toad squeezed between his hands.

He choked in disgust, his hands beginning to open to let the loathsome thing drop away; and heard a faint echo of mocking laughter that rose suddenly, and as suddenly died again. The *sidhe* had almost tricked him into letting go, he realized, but they were rejoicing too soon. He made a clutch for the slithering body of the toad, and caught it in the very last second before it slipped entirely from his fingers.

He had reached the end of his rope now, he thought as his hands closed over it again. He could not endure another thing. He shut his eyes and stood swaying on his feet, feeling horribly sick. The cold wind that had announced the coming of the *sidhe* rushed over him again, and wild, angry voices screamed in his ears. He felt a rain of blows that sent him stumbling and pitching headlong down to the rocky floor of the quarry, but something broke his fall; something strong that held him in a warm, safe grip.

Fergus opened his eyes and found he was lying on the ground looking up at his father. His father's right arm was around his shoulders. His father's left hand was firmly twined with his own right hand. The cold wind was no longer shrieking around him, but he could hear another sound; the low, anxious voice of Colm whining.

"You held on, Fergus," he heard his father saying in a voice of wonder. "*You held on!*"

He sounded as if he could hardly believe his own words, and Fergus could hardly believe them either. He gasped and swallowed hard.

"Aye," he said weakly. "I held on."

107

"Was it a very great torment they used?" MacAllister asked.

"Aye, it was terrible," Fergus admitted. "But I managed. Though mind you, I was right glad of my mother's blessing!"

"Aye, well then," MacAllister said. "You can let go of my hand now, Fergus. You have it near twisted off at the wrist with your grip!"

Fergus unlocked his fingers from their grip, then looked at both his hands. There were no burns on them, no blood from either claws or prickles, no slime from the toad's body. He held them out to his father.

"Look!" he exclaimed. "I am not hurt after all! I told myself they were not real—the snake, the fire, the wildcat; and that was true. None of them was real!"

"Your courage was real enough, if that was the kind of torment the *sidhe* put on you," MacAllister answered; "and as I am a living Highlander this moment, boy, I am proud of you. But we are not out of danger yet, remember, for we have still to reckon with An Ferla Mor!"

He rose to his full height as he spoke these words, peering up toward the lip of the quarry, and Fergus realized that he was no longer chained.

"Your chains!" he exclaimed. "What happened to them?"

"They dropped from me at the moment you fell forward into my arms," MacAllister told him. "And there they are now. Look!"

He groped around among the rocks, and straightened up with the golden chains swinging from his grip. Fergus reached out a hand to touch them.

"There is enough gold there to make everyone in the glen a rich man," he said with awe.

MacAllister laughed. "That's true," he agreed. "And there is the measure of your victory over the *sidhe*, Fergus; for I am not only going home a free man now, but a rich one as well. Come on, lad!"

He gave Fergus a hand to rise, and Colm leaped around them both and barked joyfully.

"Quiet!" MacAllister ordered, and Colm obediently stood still and soundless. "We must go now, quickly and quietly," MacAllister went on. "Are you able to walk, Fergus, or will I carry you?"

"I can walk—of course I can walk. I told you I was not hurt!" Fergus exclaimed, quite offended at the idea of being carried as if he were a baby. "But we cannot go until I have the Skeelie Woman's reward, for I promised it to her."

"Well, that is easily done," MacAllister said, smiling to himself at the offended tone. "We will take her enough jewels to light her up like a beacon if you want!"

Quickly he whipped off his ragged jacket, then spreading it on the ground he began scooping the pile of cairngorms at his feet onto it. Fergus joined in with a will, and stuffed both pockets of his breeches full too, for good measure.

"Are we ready then?" MacAllister asked, tying up the sleeves and the corners of his jacket to hold the jewels in.

"Aye, ready!" Fergus answered, patting his bulging pockets.

"Walk beside me then," MacAllister said, "and tread quieter than a cat walking, in case An Ferla Mor hears you."

Quickly and quietly then, MacAllister, Colm, and Fergus climbed out of the quarry and set off on the long walk across the mountaintop, toward the descent down the cliffs of Ben MacDui's west face. MacAllister kept the bundle of gems in his left hand, so that he could carry the golden chains slung over his right shoulder and steady them from clinking as he walked. Fergus walked by his side, and Colm padded soundlessly behind the two of them.

There was little light to guide them on their journey, for the moon was only a pale, dying face hidden behind drifts of gray cloud; but MacAllister knew the way, of course, since he had hunted so much on Ben MacDui in times past. He set a slow pace, all the same, for fear the sound of hurrying steps over the rocks would carry to the sharp hearing of An Ferla Mor. And he was careful in picking a path, so that there would be no accidental clatter of loose stones to betray them.

Whatever happened, he thought to himself as he stepped carefully along, he had to get the boy safely off the mountaintop; for it did not bear thinking about that Fergus should endure so much to rescue him, only to become the victim of An Ferla Mor in the end!

Anxiously he glanced down at the small figure keeping pace with him, and watchfully he scanned the dark wilderness of rock surrounding them. An Ferla Mor would not get the boy, he promised himself. Not while MacAllister still lived to prevent it!

An hour of this slow walking went by, and MacAllister began to think they might reach the head of the March Burn without seeing An Ferla Mor after all. Another hour passed without alarm, and his spirits rose as high as a lark singing. For the first time since he had been startled by the arrival of Colm and Fergus at the quarry, he allowed himself to think forward to the joy of seeing his beloved Peigi-Ann again.

The seven miserable years of his slavery began to slide away from him as if they had never been. He felt strong, full of life, bursting with impatience to have this slow anxious journey over so that he could begin living again in the way a man was meant to live; with a wife and a son by his side, and land of his own to till and tend. And, he told himself, with no fears of unnatural creatures like the *sidhe* to haunt him!

He glanced down for another look at Fergus, but both Fergus and Colm were trailing behind now, for MacAllister's eagerness had made him quicken his pace. He stopped walking to let the other two catch up on him, and immediately heard a strange sound in the distance. He listened, puzzling over the meaning of it, and saw Colm turn his head and prick his ears in its direction.

There were only a few yards between himself and Fergus now, and he could hear the faint noise of the boy's steps over the stones. Quickly MacAllister raised a hand to signal him to stay still, and listened for the strange sound again. It was footsteps he could hear, he realized; the kind of long, slow, heavy steps that could be made only by one creature—An Ferla Mor!

Colm growled, and instantly Fergus clapped a hand over his muzzle. It was the very signal MacAllister himself had been in the habit of using in the old hunting days when he wanted Colm to keep silence, and the old dog remembered it for he did not growl again when the hand was removed. He was still An Cu Mor, the hunting dog, now that he was out on a mountain again with his master, MacAllister thought with relief. He gave another glance at Fergus and realized that he could hear the footsteps of An Ferla Mor too, for he was standing perfectly still with his face turned to their direction.

The footsteps grew louder, drew closer. Any moment now, MacAllister thought, they would see the actual form of the creature. But if all three of them kept absolutely still, An Ferla Mor would not guess at their presence. His blind eyes would sweep over them, and he would pass them by.

112

A gleam of steely light among the rocks caught Mac-Allister's attention. The gleam was moving. It grew bigger, and flashed suddenly like a sword in the darkness. It *was* a sword, MacAllister realized. It was An Ferla Mor's sword of light, and now he could see An Ferla Mor himself!

MacAllister's mouth gaped open in astonishment at the sight, for An Ferla Mor was huge—all of twenty feet high—and he was gray all over; a great gray man made entirely of stone, with great stone legs clanking and great stone arms swinging, and great stone head turning blindly from side to side as he came surging on like part of the mountain itself bearing down on them.

Terror seized on MacAllister then—the nameless, blinding panic of terror that the Skeelie Woman had described to Fergus. He felt a wild desire to run, and run, and run, and keep on running away from the blind gray giant lurching forward like a great stone moving to crush him.

Grimly he struggled with the terror. Grimly he reminded himself of the terrible drop over The Lurcher's Crag that awaited all those who ran from An Ferla Mor, and fought with all his strength against the panic urge to do so.

But what of Fergus? The question flashed like fire across MacAllister's mind, and was immediately followed by another. Would An Ferla Mor hear the few steps that were needed for him to reach Fergus and help him fight

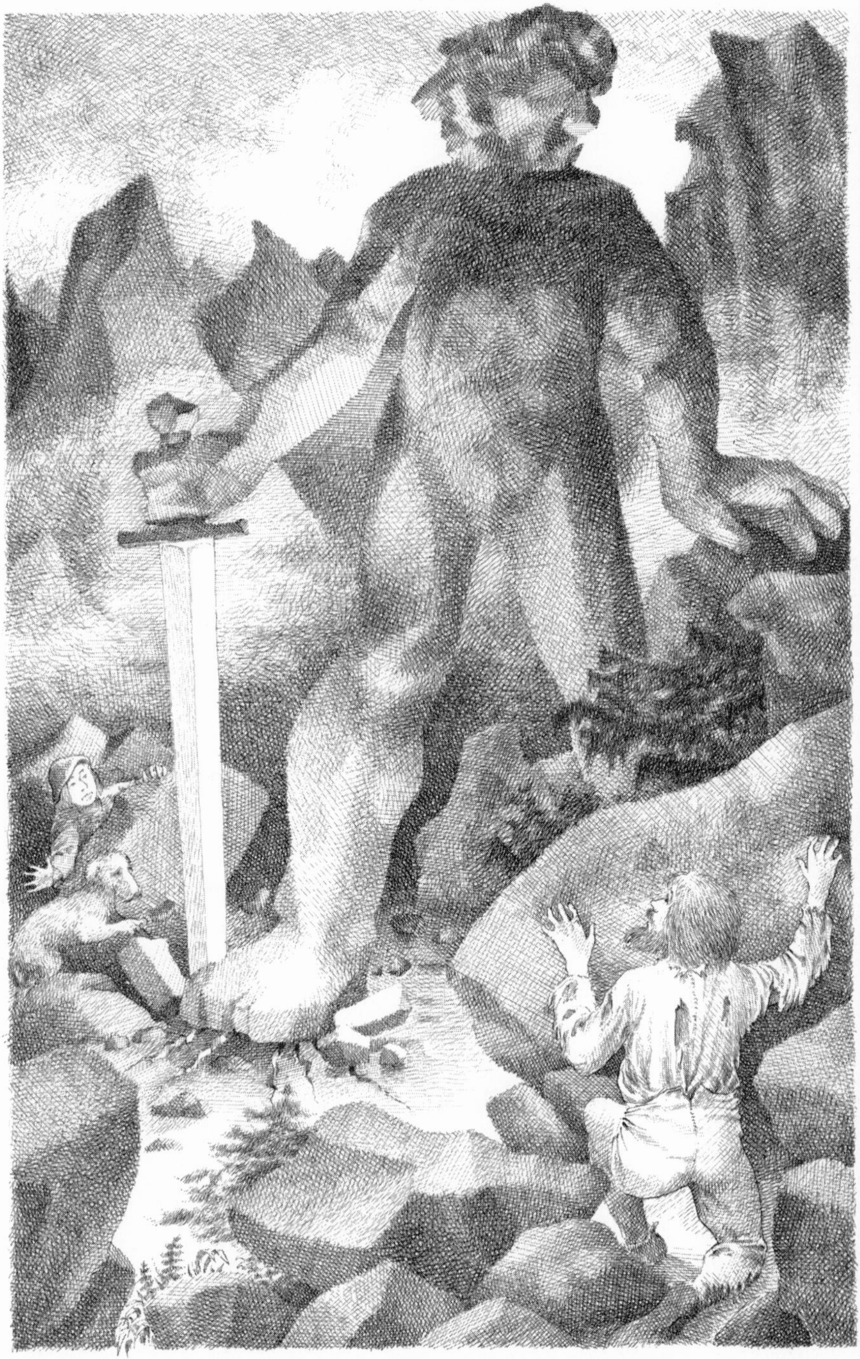

the panic that must be surging through *his* mind?

Cautiously MacAllister turned his head and took a silent step toward the crouching figures of Fergus and Colm. An Ferla Mor halted. He was only ten feet away from MacAllister and Fergus, and standing at a point midway between them. MacAllister froze in position with a foot ready for his second step. And then Fergus moved. With a cry of terror, he turned to run from An Ferla Mor, and in the same instant, several other things happened.

An Ferla Mor's sword flashed up to strike at Fergus. MacAllister tossed away the jacket in his left hand and sprang forward, roaring, with the golden chains whirling in his right hand. Colm sprang, snarling, from the other side of Fergus; and as MacAllister's falling jacket burst open to send the jewels scattering like a thousand stars of gold into the night, it was Colm's body that took the thrust of An Ferla Mor's sword.

A fraction of a second later, MacAllister had sent the golden chains whipping around An Ferla Mor's mighty form. They curled around his stone legs, around the huge tower of his body, around the great column of his neck; and as they caught, MacAllister put his own strength behind the magic power that was in them. Digging his heels into the ground he gave a tremendous heave. An Ferla Mor tottered, striking blindly out with his sword of light against MacAllister. The blade went like a flash of lightning past his ear, and then An Ferla Mor fell.

115

With a crash that seemed to shake the mountainside, the rock of his body hit the rocks underfoot. The sword of light flew out of his grasp, and like a great cat leaping, MacAllister pounced to snatch it up. In one wide flashing arc he whirled it high in the air. In one mighty stroke he brought it down, and An Ferla Mor shattered under the blow into a heap of stone that looked like any other heap of stone on the mountain.

But not quite like, MacAllister thought, staring down and recognizing the shape of the great, sightless head. Moreover, the stone of Ben MacDui was red granite and this heap of stone was gray. It would always be possible to recognize the remains of An Ferla Mor in daylight at least! He looked at the gleaming sword in his hand, and in sudden fear of the power that was in it, threw it far into the night for the *sidhe* to claim again if they chose.

Bending down then, he looked for the golden chains among the rubble that had been An Ferla Mor, but the secret force of the stroke that had destroyed him had destroyed the magic power of the chains also, and it was only garlands of withered leaves that MacAllister found there. But gold did not matter when he and Fergus were still alive and going home safe at last, he told himself triumphantly. Then he remembered Colm.

Quickly then, MacAllister swung around to look for the old dog, and saw Fergus crouched on the ground with Colm's head cradled on his knees. MacAllister stepped

116

toward him, and knelt down to put his hand on the creature's heart.

"He saved me," Fergus said, and he was weeping as he spoke. "I thought he was too old to be of any use to me, but the Skeelie Woman said, '*The day of An Cu Mor is not yet over*,' and she was right. He saved me from An Ferla Mor. And now he is dying."

There was still a very faint heartbeat under Colm's rough gray coat, for deep as the sword of light had pierced, a strong creature like An Cu Mor dies hard. MacAllister put one arm around Fergus and kept his other hand on Colm until the heartbeat finally stopped; then gently he said,

"The day of An Cu Mor is over now, Fergus."

Slowly Fergus laid Colm's head down, and slowly he rose to his feet. "I do not remember a time without Colm," he said. "How can we leave him here like this!"

MacAllister measured the great weight of Colm's body with his eye. "We will not leave him," MacAllister answered. "We will all go home together."

He bent down, and with a mighty effort, gathered Colm into his strong arms. Fergus walked beside him as he stepped forward holding the weight of the body supported against his chest. And so began the last part of their journey home.

9

COLM'S CROFT

MacAllister carried Colm's body by himself all the way to the point where the March Burn tumbled over the cliffs. He scrambled down the cliffs still holding it without any help from Fergus; but when they reached the foot of the cliffs and Fergus unhitched his pony, he laid Colm's body across the front of the saddle and told Fergus to mount behind it. Fergus took the reins and MacAllister walked beside the pony as they began traveling north then, homeward through the Lairig Ghru.

It was a sad journey that, and a weary one too, for Fergus was tired to the bone by this time and MacAllister himself was not in much better case. As dawn brought light into the sky, however, and as they drew nearer and nearer to their own glen, both MacAllister and Fergus felt the weariness drop from them. Fergus sat up straight in the saddle again. MacAllister strode along with his head up, eagerly scanning the way ahead, and a high tide of joy rose in him when he caught the first longed-for sight of his own glen at last.

"It will not be long now!" he exclaimed, thinking of Peigi-Ann and wondering—as he had wondered every day of his long slavery—what the years of sorrow had done to her.

"Aye, half an hour will bring us home," Fergus agreed, thinking of Peigi-Ann also, and wondering who would reach her first with news of their coming, for it seemed that the whole glen was awake to watch it.

Everywhere now he could see signs of the stir it was causing. A shepherd on the skyline waved and whistled to them. Other figures waved and called from the doorways of the little houses that dotted the hillslopes on either side of them. In the distance he could see boys and men running, waving their arms and shouting with excitement as they carried the news to those in the houses further down the glen.

His mother would be on the doorstep to greet them, Fergus thought with a smile. And he was right, for when they came in sight of their own house he could see a patch of blue in the doorway, which meant that Peigi-Ann was there, wearing her best dress that had a collar of fine lace on it and was the same deep blue as her beautiful eyes.

"*Peigi-Ann!*" MacAllister shouted, and broke into a run.

She met him halfway to the house, calling out, laugh-

119

ing, crying, all in the one breath, and they clung together like two drowning people who have nothing left in the world to hold on to but one another.

Fergus dismounted beside them, nearly falling off his pony with weariness, and was swept into the same embrace. Murdo came up with his face one vast beam of delight, and shook MacAllister's hand as hard as if it were the well handle and he pumping up enough water to last a week.

Neighbor after neighbor arrived, until the crowd around them was growing so fast it seemed people were springing up out of the very ground to swell it. Then, in the midst of all the shouting and laughing and handshaking, Peigi-Ann saw the body of Colm over the saddle of the pony and her tears of joy turned to tears of sorrow.

"He was old. He would have died soon anyway," Mac-Allister said, trying to comfort her. "We will give him decent burial here at home, Peigi-Ann, among those who loved him. And you have this to be grateful for, at least; that he was killed in saving Fergus from An Ferla Mor."

"I told you the day of An Cu Mor was not yet over," a voice said, and the Skeelie Woman stepped forward from the crowd of neighbors. MacAllister turned to her, and the Skeelie Woman told him,

"You have held out against the *sidhe* for over thirteen years now, MacAllister, and seven of those have been spent in slavery. But there comes a time when even the most stubborn of men must listen to advice; and so, will you listen to one last wise word from me?"

"Yes, I will listen," MacAllister agreed. "Although that does not mean I will do as you say."

"Then hear this," the Skeelie Woman told him, "for I know the ways of the *sidhe* better than anyone here. There is only one way you can finally defeat their claim to the Goodman's Croft, MacAllister. You must give that piece of land the sacrifice of blood which land always demands of a man before it can become truly his, and his alone, for all time and forever. You must give it the heart of a creature that is dear to your own heart."

MacAllister stared in horror at her. "What kind of talk is this?" he demanded, and put his arms around Peigi-Ann and Fergus as if to protect them. "How can I give the land the heart of a creature dear to me?"

"Bury Colm in the Goodman's Croft," the Skeelie Woman said quietly. "He gave his life freely against An Ferla Mor, who was the creature of the *sidhe*. Now let the blood of An Cu Mor be the sacrifice that breaks their power forever."

MacAllister looked long at the Skeelie Woman and saw truth in her strange eyes. "Yes," he said at last. "I will do that." He turned to Fergus and ordered, "Fetch me a spade, boy."

"I have something to give to the Skeelie Woman first," said Fergus, and he began digging in his pockets for the cairngorms he had put there. The Skeelie Woman held out her apron to receive them, her eyes gleaming with greed now.

"You asked for a double handful," Fergus said, pouring the golden gems into her apron, "and that is what I have here."

"Aieee! Aieee! You are a clever boy, Fergus!" the Skeelie Woman crooned, watching the glitter of them. "Aieee, I will walk in beauty yet before I die!"

Away she went then, with love and greed shining out of her shriveled brown face and the stones clutched in her apron. Fergus and MacAllister watched her gaudy little figure out of sight, then Fergus fetched a spade and Mac-Allister buried Colm deep in the soil of the Goodman's Croft.

"We will call it Colm's Croft, now," he told Peigi-Ann and Fergus when he had finished patting the earth smooth over the spot where Colm lay buried. "And later today, Murdo will help me to tear out that hedge of rowan and elder, and I will plow the land."

"No!" Fergus exclaimed. "*I* will plow the land. I have earned the right to do that, have I not?"

MacAllister looked at Peigi-Ann. Then he looked at Fergus, and he laughed. "You have indeed," he agreed.

And so later that day, when there had been time for some of their rejoicing to settle, Murdo and MacAllister tore out the hedge of rowan and elder and Fergus plowed the land that was now Colm's Croft. MacAllister and Peigi-Ann stood hand in hand watching him, and when the plowing was finished, MacAllister told them both,

"I will plant barley there this year."

"You will not!" said Peigi-Ann. "*I* will plant Colm's Croft."

"You?" MacAllister exclaimed, and Peigi-Ann nodded.

"Yes," said she, "and I will choose what to put in it."

"And what will that be?" MacAllister asked, wondering what on earth was in her mind.

Peigi-Ann looked lovingly at Colm's Croft, and her voice was tender when she spoke. "I will make a garden of this little patch of ground," she told MacAllister. "I will grow pearlwort in it, for faithfulness; and woodbine, that guards against grief. I will grow thyme in it, and St. John's Wort, and every kind of plant that has a power of healing illness. I will grow roses in it for their color and their sweet scent to remind me that nothing but beauty and loving kindness should spring from the noble heart of An Cu Mor."

"You are right," MacAllister said soberly. "It was my stubborn nature that began all this, and we have suffered much because of it. But good will come out of it in the end if you make this ground a remembrance to Colm, and so your way is the right way now."

"I will weed the ground for you," Fergus promised his mother, smiling with the pleasure her idea had given him.

"And I will see that you never lack for plants to put in it," MacAllister added.

Then he put his arm around Peigi-Ann while they all went back to the house together talking happily of Colm's Croft, and the next day Peigi-Ann began making the little garden she had planned.

It was a long time in the making, for although her plants were all humble ones she chose them with loving care and every single one of them flourished. There was many a person after that had cause to be grateful for their healing powers, and so the name of Colm became cherished in the glen. Moreover, both she and MacAllister lived to a ripe old age to watch the garden grow into a remembrance of him; and they loved one another until they died.

The Skeelie Woman, also, proved to be right in all she had said, for the *sidhe* never troubled MacAllister again over his land. From that day forward, therefore, he farmed it as a man should; in peace and quietness and with much honest toil. Then Fergus farmed the land and tended the little garden also, and his son did the same after him, and his son's son after that. But the great-grandson of Fergus decided to leave the farm to try for his fortune in America, and he was the last of the MacAllisters in that glen.

The farm quickly became a ruin once he had gone; but there was a strange thing happened with Colm's Croft, for although the grass and the heather spread everywhere else, no weed ever grew in that little patch of ground. The plants set there by the loving hands of Peigi-Ann still kept opening and flowering brightly in their season. A gentle hum of honeybees hung always over them in the months of sun and summer. And still, it is said, there is no spot in all the Highlands so beautiful or so peaceful as the little garden that sprang from the noble heart of An Cu Mor.

And that is all there is to tell of MacAllister's story. It is not the end of the story of Ben MacDui, however, for the creature that roams there to this day is the ghost of An Ferla Mor searching, always searching for the lost treasure of the *sidhe*. But this ghost is blind, of course, as An Ferla Mor himself was blind, and so it can never find the jewels MacAllister flung away on the night he sprang to the help of Fergus.

The ghost guards the mountain, for all that, in the same fearful way that An Ferla Mor guarded it; as many and many a person has had cause to tell since then. Some of these, moreover, are well-known mountaineers whose word cannot be doubted, and they are all agreed on one thing.

The mere sight of Ben MacDui's Great Gray Man, they say, is enough to send the bravest person running in terror down the mountainside, *but it is not toward safety that he runs*! The place he heads for in his panic is The

Lurcher's Crag, and there are men living today who have been saved in the very nick of time from plunging to death over that terrible cliff. And that really is the end of the story—except for one last thing.

The heap of gray stone that was once An Ferla Mor is easy to see among the red granite rock of Ben MacDui, and the lost jewels still lie where they fell around it. The gleaming gold of them among the rocks is easy to see too, and anyone who chooses may climb the mountain to gather them.

However, it would have to be a very brave person indeed who did this, and he would certainly have to keep a very strict lookout for the ghost of An Ferla Mor if he wanted to come home safe again. And so the chances are that the jewels will lie there forever and always; and that forever and always also, the ghost of An Ferla Mor will be searching for them and Ben MacDui will be a haunted mountain.

Format by Kohar Alexanian

Set in 12 point Caslon Old Face

Composed and bound by American Book–Stratford Press, Inc.

Printed by The Murray Printing Co.

HARPER & ROW, PUBLISHERS, INC.